Starstruck

Lisa Cherie

ISBN
978-1-963254-18-1 (Paperback)
978-1-963254-19-8 (eBook)
978-1-963254-17-4 (Hardcover)

Starstruck

To my friends and family who always asked for the next chapter.

Chapter One

$\mathcal{L}$aura sat in her living room, watching *Entertainment Update* where the latest news on new movies and the entertainment industry were discussed. She sat in shock watching them interview the newest heartthrob, who apparently had not been prepped beforehand. She shook her head at some of his responses. While not bad, they weren't always thought through before answering. It was obvious that he hadn't been coached at all. He just said whatever came to mind and laughed a lot. He was extremely uncomfortable. And cute. Actually, when he mussed his hair, he was sexy. She laughed to herself as she listened to another of his replies. He was shocked at the reactions to him. *"They were screaming. I am not sure why. They didn't seem to care what I was saying. They just kept screaming. I know it's not me, it is the character. It's just so bizarre."* Sebastian was telling the interviewer. They had caught him after a convention where apparently several thousand fans had shown up to see the cast of the upcoming movie *Royalty Unknown*.

No, not the character. It's you, she thought. At least for some of us. Her phone rang and she grabbed it quickly. "Hello." She turned her attention back to the screen, not wanting to miss anything that was being said. Her attentive gaze traveled over his attire, taking in the black jeans and red button-down shirt. He kept running his hands through his chestnut brown hair in a nervous gesture and the disheveled look just made him more attractive.

"Are you watching this?" her best friend Mandy asked. "Yes." Answered Laura. "He looks so nervous. He is so cute." "Did you send the e-mail?" Mandy asked.

"No." Laura glanced at her laptop, sitting on the coffee table. Sebastian's web page was pulled up on the screen.

"Just send it." Urged Mandy. "I'm sure he'll appreciate getting something positive from one of his fans."

Laura glanced back at the screen on the television and then grabbed her computer from the table. She only gave herself a brief moment to think about it. She knew she would back out if she thought too long.

After finding his personal web page, she had felt like she should send him something to let him know that not everyone was disappointed by him being chosen for the role of Simon. Laura had mentioned to Mandy about sending him a message of reassurance, although she knew he wouldn't need that from someone like her. Mandy had eagerly agreed that she should write him. Then Laura hadn't sent the message, so Mandy had been bugging her about it for the last couple of days. They both knew that he had been getting more than his share of hate mail.

Laura glanced at the television screen. If she were honest with herself, she had just felt the need to make some kind of contact with him. Even knowing that odds of getting any kind of response back from him were against her. She was sure that he was busy enough without having time to read his e-mails. She had had second thoughts and now she was overanalyzing. She shook her head. She knew that if she didn't do it now, she never would. She sighed. This was one of those times when she knew that if she didn't, she would always wonder– what if she had? Not only that, but Mandy would probably keep bugging her until she broke down and sent the message, anyway.

Sebastian,

I know that you are terribly busy filming your movies, but I hope you have time to check your mail. I just wanted to let you know that I think you are the perfect choice for the part of Simon. Don't let what others are saying, get to you. People go kind of crazy about fictional characters sometimes and it gets ridiculous. I also had to tell you that I don't think that it is just the character that has everyone's attention. I know for me; I appreciate your openness and honesty during your interviews. Your hair is amazing, and your accent is extremely sexy. Not to say that the rest of you isn't. Those things just stand out to me. I am sure that you don't need someone like me, who is way out of your league, to tell you these things. I just felt that after watching your interview and hearing your comment about your inadequacies, I should say something. Well, I know that you are very busy, so I won't take up any more of your time. If you happen to think of your fans, maybe this message some time during an interview, just smile one of those sexy smiles for me. LOL.

Laura

She quickly hit send before she could question what she was doing and closed her e-mail. Well, that's done. Can't take it back now. She smiled. Hopefully, he would get a chance to read it instead of all of the rude e-mails he had been receiving from others. It seemed that some of the fans of the storyline for the part he was cast in, had already decided who they thought should have the part and were being extremely vocal about their displeasure. People just didn't understand how casting, and such worked for movies. It wasn't like the fans could vote their favorite actors and actresses into the roles that they wanted them to have.

"It's sent." Laura told Mandy. Mandy had been her best friend since grade school, and they had been inseparable growing up. Usually, if Laura got into trouble, then Mandy was with her. Mandy had a way of talking Laura into doing things that she wouldn't normally do on her own.

Mandy squealed loudly in her ear. "Great! He is so gorgeous." She sighed.

Laura laughed at her friend. "You live in Los Angeles. Why don't you go and meet him?"

Mandy laughed. "Ha! Ha! You are funny. I don't frequent the places he does. Besides, I couldn't afford to on my salary, anyway."

"How is your job? Is Victoria nicer now?" asked Laura. Her friend worked for one of the popular papers in Los Angeles and she and her boss seemed to disagree often.

"We're getting along much better. I've gotten a few good stories for her, lately, so she's laid off."

"That's great." Laura said sincerely. She had watched her friend work hard to build her career the last few years and she wanted her to be happy. Mandy really loved what she did and would be much happier if it weren't for the tension between her and her boss. Laura turned off her television as the show ended and sat back on the couch, stretching out her long legs and propping her feet up on the coffee table in front of her. She set her laptop on the couch beside her.

"It probably won't last, but we'll see." Said Mandy.

"Don't say that. Think positive." Laura scolded, playfully.

"Yes, mom." Said Mandy, laughing. "Oh, I've got to go. I have an interview in an hour. I'll talk to you soon."

"Okay. Talk to you later." Answered Laura. She was used to the quick conversations that she had with Mandy. They talked three or four times a week, but for short periods of time. They caught up and kept in touch and that is what mattered. She glanced at her watch and then went back to her computer. She could get some work done before she went to bed.

--- ❦ ---

Laura stepped in the front door of *Little Italy* and glanced around. The dimly lit restaurant had a handful of customers and you could hear the low murmur of conversations. The hostess, Amber, smiled and greeted her. "Table for one?"

Laura nodded. "Yes, the usual, please, if it's available."

Amber nodded, used to Laura's request considering that she visited regularly. "Follow me, please."

Laura followed her to a booth in the back corner. She slid into one side and sat her bag on the seat beside her. "Thank you."

Amber smiled and handed her a menu. "Your waiter will be with you in a minute."

A few minutes later, the waiter appeared at her table. "Laura." He said as he slid into the booth across from her. He smiled at her. "Mama and Papa will be happy to see you."

"Marco." Laura smiled at the dark-haired waiter sitting across from her. "You know I have to have Mama's food at least once a week."

Marco laughed. "Yes, you do. The lasagna, right?" He winked at her as she narrowed her eyes at him, and he slid out of the booth. "I know, I know. You want the manicotti and a house salad with Mama's famous dressing. Wine?"

Laura shook her head. "Not tonight, thank you. Water will be fine."

"Be right out." Marco bowed slightly and left.

Laura laughed at his antics and turned her attention to her bag. She pulled out the script for *Dawn's Cover* and began reading it. She worked at a talent agency and they were getting ready to film *Dawn's Cover*, so she wanted to make sure that she knew the script inside and out.

--- ❦ ---

The next morning, Laura grabbed a stack of papers off the fax machine and flipped through them. Ever since the word had gotten out about the filming of the upcoming movie, they had been getting tons of resumes faxed and mailed in. She started sorting them by position being applied for. Laura was the office manager for Matt Logan who owned *Studio B* Talent Agency.

The phone rang and she grabbed it. "Good Morning, *Studio B*."

"Hi, Laura. This is Donna. Is Matt available?"

Laura glanced at the lights on the phone console. "He's on the other line. Can I give him a message?"

"Sure. I need three models for a beach shoot this weekend. Two females and one male. Just tell him to give me a call if he's got someone available."

Laura wrote down the details. "Okay, Donna. No problem. I'll have him call you."

"Are you available, Laura?" asked Donna.

Laura stood still for a moment, thrown off guard, then shook her head. "No. Sorry, Donna. You know I don't model anymore."

"You did a shoot for Matt a couple months back." Insisted Donna.

"Yes, but that was a fill in." she sighed. It had been six years and they still tried to talk her into doing jobs. "I'll have Matt call you."

"Thanks, Laura."

Laura hung up the phone and dropped into her chair. She glanced at the picture of her and Mandy on her desk. She wished her friend lived closer. It didn't seem to get any easier when people kept reminding her of her old career.

- - - ∽ - - -

Sebastian walked in the front door, turned on the light and sighed. So far. So good. No one seemed to know where he was. Things had gotten more intense after this last movie. Some people were upset about him being cast as the lead role in *Royalty Unknown*. Others did not seem to mind. Regardless, he just wanted to have some privacy for a brief time. He walked through the living room to the guest room down the hall. One of his friends owned the beach house and had given him the keys to stay there. His friend was busy out of town working on a movie, so the house was empty. He flipped on the bedroom light and set his duffel bag on the bed. He set his laptop bag on the chair by the dresser, then went into the bathroom to take a shower.

An hour later, after his shower and eating, he felt much better and pulled out his laptop and set it up. He hadn't checked his e-mail in a while and decided to do that before going to bed for the night. He signed in and sighed at the amount of mail that was in his box. The subject lines were varied, but similar. <u>Please reply.</u>, <u>Will you marry me?</u>, <u>Will you meet me for dinner?</u>, <u>I love you</u>, <u>I'm your biggest fan</u>, <u>You are so hot</u>, <u>Will you go on a date with me?</u> Sebastian smiled to himself as he read through his mail. There was no way possible to reply to everyone. Should he reply to any of them? He continued to flip through the pages and scrolled through the messages, reading some occasionally. <u>Not a screaming teenager</u>. Hmm. That sounded interesting. He opened it and read the message.

> *Sebastian,*
>
> I know that you are terribly busy filming your movies, but I hope you have time to check your mail. I just wanted to let you know that I think you are the perfect choice for the part of Simon. Don't let what others are saying, get to you. People go kind of crazy about fictional characters sometimes and it gets ridiculous. I also had to tell you that I don't think that it is just the character that has everyone's attention. I know for me; I appreciate your openness and honesty during your interviews. Your hair is amazing, and your accent is extremely sexy. Not to say that the rest of you isn't. Those things just

stand out to me. I am sure that you don't need someone like me, who is way out of your league to tell you these things. I just felt that after watching your interview and hearing your comment about your inadequacies, I should say something. Well, I know that you are very busy, so I won't take up any more of your time. If you happen to think of your fans, maybe this message some time during an interview, just smile one of those sexy smiles for me. LOL.

Laura

That was an intriguing message. No begging for an autograph or a date. No claim to be the biggest fan. Just a straightforward, nice message. She even sounded intelligent. Not a screaming teenager, indeed. Out of his league? He did not like the sound of that. He was certainly no better than anyone else. How to get that point across? His e-mail flashed a new message and he read it. Of course, the interview on Wednesday night. He typed a quick message and hit send.

- - - ༽ - - -

Over the last couple of days, Laura had stayed busy at work and hadn't gotten home until late. She had checked her e-mail every night and sifted through the numerous junk mail that seemed to multiply every day. She never found anything of interest until a week later. She was winding down for the evening and turned on the television and then booted up her laptop and set it on her lap. It was her usual routine. She didn't watch much television but liked to have some sound in the background.

While checking her e-mail, she found an unexpected message. It didn't seem likely, but he was listed as the sender. Probably someone was answering his mail for him.

Laura,

Thank you for the message. Thank you for the compliments. Sexy, huh? I figured that is mostly coming from the movie character. I appreciate your sentiments otherwise. I do not think that anyone is out of my league. We are all people. Some do different things. I act. That does not make me any better than anyone else. I am glad that you enjoy my interviews. I do think of my fans when I am talking. Maybe that is what makes me nervous. I think everyone has inadequacies.

They are just not on show for the whole world to see. I do appreciate your message and I am never too busy to respond to a fan. Feel free to e-mail me again. I enjoyed receiving your message and I mean that sincerely. Oh, and if you get the chance to catch my interview tonight on *Entertainment Update*, I will be thinking of you and send that smile your way. 5 PM. You will know it is for you. I promise.

Sebastian

Laura glanced at her watch, 8:15. California was three hours behind, so *Entertainment Update* would be on now. Had she already missed the interview? She flipped the channel and turned up the volume. *"When we return, we'll be talking to Sebastian Thomas about his role in the upcoming movie Royalty Unknown."*

She watched the commercials patiently. What was he going to do? She laughed at herself. Probably, nothing special. Just throw out one of those sexy smiles to the camera.

Entertainment Update came back on and Laura sat riveted to the program.

EU: Hi. I'm Marla Snow and we have Sebastian Thomas with us tonight. (The petite hostess turned her attention to Sebastian who was sitting in a chair next to her.) Sebastian, we are pleased you could join us tonight.

S: Thank you for having me on the show.

EU: (Marla smiled). Your fans are eager to hear about your new movie.

S: (Sebastian laughed). I think most of my fans already know about my new movie.

EU: (Marla laughed). Yes, they do keep track of you. Tell me though, how do you handle the upset fans?

S: I do not really deal with them. I have never met any personally. Usually it is just hate mail and I stop reading after the first sentence.

EU: So, you don't read your fan mail?

S: I read my fan mail. I do not read the hate mail.

EU: How do you tell the difference? Does someone read your mail for you?

S: No. I read my mail. If the mail gets nasty after the first few sentences, then I quit reading it.

Laura smiled as the petite blonde squirmed in her seat. That is what you get for trying to put him on the spot, she thought.

EU: Has the mail from the upset fans died down? I've seen some of the previews for your movie and you seem to fit the part well.

S: (Sebastian nodded.) Thank you, Marla. I have gotten some mail from others that say that they can't wait to see the movie. Some date requests.

EU: Date requests, huh? Any marriage proposals?

S: (Sebastian smiled.) I have gotten a couple of those.

EU: (Marla smiled and fluttered her lashes flirtatiously at him). I bet you have.

Sebastian glanced uncomfortably at the table in front of him and grabbed his glass of water and took a drink.

EU: Tell us about your movie. (Prompted Marla)

S: It is about a man and a woman that meet by accident and are attracted to each other, but do not know who the other is. They run into each other, again a couple of times before they finally introduce themselves. They fall in love, but there is a huge secret between them. He is a prince, but she does not know that when they meet, and he does not tell her because he wants her to like him for himself.

EU: Sounds interesting. We have a clip of the show. Let's take a look.

Sebastian nodded and they both turned their attention to a screen to their left.

Someone stopped in front of her and grabbed her hand. "Care to dance?"

Isabelle looked up in surprise as the lead singer of the band on stage led her onto the dance floor.

They danced quietly for a few moments, staring into each other's eyes before either could say anything.

"I remember you." He said.

"You do?" asked Isabelle.

"You were standing on the sidewalk. You saved me."

"Saved you?"

He shook his head. "It's not important. Why were you standing on the sidewalk that day?"

"I was on my way to try on a dress for my best friend's wedding."

The music stopped and they vaguely heard the clatter of the instruments being put away.

It seemed only a few brief minutes before they heard anyone.

"Hey, man. We've got to run." One of the guys said from the stage.

Simon nodded in acknowledgement and smiled, then leaned towards Isabelle and kissed her. It felt the same as before. Electricity arced between them. Too soon he pulled away. "Thank you for the dance." Then he walked towards the stage and left.

Isabelle stood on the dance floor in a daze as her friends rushed up to her.

EU: That was hot! (Marla exclaimed.)

Sebastian laughed self-consciously and Marla smiled flirtatiously at him.

EU: Last question. (She glanced at a card that she was holding) This one is from a fan— She wants to know what your favorite scene of the movie is.

S: Well, (Sebastian glanced around briefly) I don't know of one in particular. I did have fun singing on stage, though.

EU: That was great. Was that you or were you lip-syncing?

S: (Sebastian shook his head.) No. That was me singing.

EU: You and Karla looked kind of close there. Was that chemistry just on screen or should we expect to see you two off screen together?

S: (Sebastian chuckled) No. That was strictly acting. Karla and I are only friends.

EU: I thought we might actually see you with a woman on your arm at the next event.

S: No.

EU: (Marla smiled at the camera.) Well, you heard him ladies, he is still single. (She turned back to Sebastian) Okay. That's all we have time for. Anything you want to say to your fans?

S: Actually, yes. (Sebastian smiled and turned towards the camera.) This is for Laura. (He smiled that sexy smile that melted hearts everywhere and blew a kiss to the camera). And you are definitely not out of my league.

The audience went crazy and a commercial came on to the television. Laura sat on the couch in astonishment with a silly smile on her face. He was so crazy. Now he had stirred up all kinds of gossip.

The show came back on and Marla was sitting on stage alone, smiling. *"Now I guess Sebastian's fans have something else to ponder. Who is the mysterious Laura? His girlfriend?"*

Laura just sat listening to Marla talk. None of what she said really registered. She was enjoying her moment. She laughed as she got up from the couch and went to take a shower. Now he had really started something.

--- ❦ ---

After her shower, Laura slipped into some comfy lounge pants and a tank top and sat down at her computer. Out of curiosity, she did a search on Sebastian Thomas.

<u>Who is Laura?</u> Laura clicked on the link. That hadn't taken very long. There was even a replay of the final part of the interview. Laura read through the posts.

<u>Has anyone ever heard him speak of her before?</u> <u>She is not one of the cast members.</u>

<u>I thought he was single. I'm supposed to marry him. Has anyone seen him out with anyone?</u>

<u>The Mysterious Laura who is she?</u>

<u>Do you think she's pretty? She would have to be to get a guy like him. He can't be attached; he's supposed to be single.</u>

<u>I am devastated, we were supposed to meet and fall in love. Does anyone know who Laura is?</u>

<u>Do you think he's serious about Laura?</u>

Later that evening, Laura was finishing up some research on her computer, when she received a message. She glanced at the clock and decided to check it before going to bed. She clicked on her inbox.

Laura,

Did you catch the interview?

Sebastian

She shook her head and laughed. She hadn't expected to hear from him, again. She had been surprised to receive the last message. She knew he must get some ridiculous amount of e-mail and it would be crazy to try to respond to any or even all of it. How had he managed to choose hers out of all of the others to respond to?

Sebastian,

I saw it. Are you crazy? Have you checked the message boards? Everyone is trying to figure out who Laura is. I hope that's your girlfriend's name, too.

Laura

Laura,

LOL. You know I do not have a girlfriend. That was for you.

Sebastian

Sebastian,

If you thought you had hate mail before, you are in for it now. I am sure that you have some disappointed fans tonight. They were hoping to marry you. Now they think there is someone else in your life. The mysterious Laura.

Laura

After a while, they just started typing quick messages back and forth.

S: Yes. Who is the mysterious Laura?

L: Just an everyday person, who enjoys your movies and thinks you are sexy like at least half of the population. Nothing special. Nothing mysterious.

S: I think you are wrong there. You are something special. You got my attention.

L: I just sent you a message like probably thousands of other people.

S: Yes, but yours caught my attention. Made me curious about the person who wrote it.

L: I appreciate that, but we both know that if I were in front of you asking for an autograph, you wouldn't notice me from anyone else.

S: Somehow, I think I would.

L: Thanks for the flattery, but I'm not some star struck fan. Not one of the teens who scream and cry when they see you.

S: That is what I like about you. You are honest and up front. You treat me like a normal person. Not someone put up on a pedestal.

L: Yeah, I send e-mails to guys all the time and tell them how sexy I think they are. **Not really**.

S: Why **did** you do that?

L: I told you that in the message. I thought you should at least get a positive e-mail not entirely associated with your character and not from a screaming teen begging for you to marry them and give them children.

S: LOL. I do get some of those. I got a proposal the other day.

L: Is that the one that you responded to in your interview?

S: Yes. I treated it as a joke.

L: I could tell. Even though, you were so serious at first.

S: I have to be careful that I do not offend anyone.

L: Yes. I can understand that.

S: Back to you. You are not a screaming teen, so how old are you? Am I allowed to ask that?

L: Twenty-four

S: Oh. My age. Interesting. I am intrigued.

L: Maybe so, but I am smart enough to know that you are out of my league.

S: I do not like it when you say that. I am not out of your league.

L: It is the truth.

S: In your eyes.

L: And the rest of the world's.

S: I doubt that.

L: LOL. If you showed up at an event with me on your arm, people would go crazy.

S: Let's try it and see.

L: No thank you. That was just an example.

S: I am anxious to meet you.

L: You're too busy. I'd better run. I need to get some rest for tomorrow. I enjoyed talking to you. Good night.

Laura signed off her computer and climbed into bed before she could think about what she had just done. She tossed and turned, finally falling asleep only to dream of Sebastian's blue eyes.

Chapter Two

Laura woke the next morning before her alarm went off and got ready for work. She glanced at the clock on her way to the front door. 7:30. Well, she would be extra early today. She grabbed her bag and purse and left her apartment, locking the door behind her. She smiled to herself as she walked to her car. She had left the apartment without touching her computer. She felt bad about her abruptness the night before and wanted to apologize, but she could do it later.

Laura stopped by the post office and picked up the mail from the post office box that Matt had rented for *Studio B*, then drove through a drive thru and ordered a couple bagels and a mocha latte, then drove to the office. She entered through the back door and headed straight to the front to her desk. She had been the office manager for Matt for over five years and usually arrived before him and opened up for the day. She got settled and glanced around thinking about what she needed to do. She finished her bagel and started sorting the mail. Her thoughts straying to the scene they had shown of Sebastian the other night from his movie. Only it was her in his arms, dancing.

"You're here early."

Laura jumped and dumped the stack of mail on the floor. "Don't sneak up on me like that." She scolded Matt as she dropped to the floor to pick up the mail.

Matt laughed. "I thought you heard me come in. I wasn't quiet. You know, I never am."

Laura scowled at him as she put the mail back on her desk. "No, you never are quiet." She grabbed a bag off her desk. "Here I got you a bagel."

Matt took the bag and peeked inside. "Ahh. A woman after my heart. Sure, you won't marry me?"

Laura frowned at him. "Right. You'd better get that ring on Elizabeth's finger."

Matt smiled widely. "I picked one out the other day."

"Well, let me see it." Laura followed him to his office, happy to be distracted from her thoughts of Sebastian.

Matt pulled the black velvet box out of his briefcase and held it out to her. "Tell me what you think."

Laura opened the box to reveal a 14-karat gold ring with a 2-carat diamond in the center, surrounded by smaller diamonds. "Wow!"

"Do you think she'll like it?"

"Of course." answered Laura. "It's beautiful. When are you going to ask her?"

"After we're finished with this movie."

"Just the casting, right?"

Matt shook his head. "No. The filming and everything. I won't have time to do anything but breathe this movie. You know how it is. You've been through several movies with me. I want to be able to spend time with Elizabeth."

Laura nodded. "I understand what you are saying, but I just don't think that you should wait so long."

The doorbell rang and Matt glanced at his watch. "We don't have time for this right now. That's Lance Stevens, the writer for *Dawn's Cover*. We are reviewing some files today before the casting call next Saturday." He grabbed his notebook from his briefcase. "I need you to pull these files for me, please."

Laura took the list from him and glanced over it. "Yes sir." She'd let him get away with changing the subject for now. She walked back to the front of the office and unlocked the door to let Lance in. She was glad that they had installed the doorbell. That way, if appointments showed early, they would know that they had arrived even if the office wasn't unlocked, yet.

"Hi, Laura." Greeted Lance.

"Good morning, Lance. Are you ready for the chaos?" Responded Laura.

"Definitely. I can't wait to see my script on the big screen. This will be great."

Laura laughed. "Tell me that in a couple of weeks." She walked behind her desk and over to the file cabinets. "Matt's in his office. I'll put the files in the conference room."

Laura started pulling files out of the drawers and answering phone calls. The day sped by and when she looked at the clock, again, it was after 7:00 p.m.

Matt walked out of the conference room and glanced up at her from the paper he was reading. "What are you still doing here?"

"I had things to finish."

"You need to go home. I need you rested. Things are going to be crazy around here. Tomorrow's Friday and I want to get everything set up for next week. We have people coming in to interview for the tech positions early next week and then the casting call is next Saturday."

"Don't worry, Matt. I will be fine. I'm leaving now and I'll see you at nine tomorrow. Okay?"

Matt nodded. "I'm starting already?"

Laura smiled at him. "I can handle it. You go home soon. I need you rested, too." She grabbed her bag and her purse and headed for the back door. "See you tomorrow Lance."

Laura drove straight home and went straight to the shower. Her stomach started growling as she was slipping into yoga pants and a tank top. She went to the kitchen and prepared herself a salad, then sat down with her laptop on the couch. Time to type an apology. She'd felt bad all day. She wasn't a rude person by nature, and she had to apologize. Well, at least he probably wouldn't mention them meeting, again. She pulled up her e-mail and typed a message.

Sebastian,

I'm not sure if you'll even want to read this message after my rude behavior, but I wanted to apologize. I'm sorry for practically hanging up on you last night. I am just trying to keep myself grounded. I know how busy your life probably is with filming and promotion of your films and I know how crazy things get. Anyway, I just wanted to say I'm sorry for being rude.

Laura

She hit send and started sifting through her e-mail, deleting twenty- five messages at a time. So much garbage. It was worse than what she got in her regular mailbox. Her phone rang and she answered it before it could ring, again. "Hello, Mandy."

"I hate it when you do that." Said Mandy. "What are you doing?"

"Checking e-mail." Answered Laura.

"He was talking about you last night, wasn't he?" asked Mandy.

Laura stopped scanning her messages. "What?" She didn't have a clue what her friend was talking about.

Mandy sighed. "Listen to me. Stop reading your e-mail. Sebastian was interviewed on *Entertainment Update* last night. At the end, he was talking about you. He sent that kiss to you."

Laura smiled as she remembered that sexy smile and kiss. Of course, Mandy would have seen it. She didn't miss anything that she could that was related to Sebastian Thomas or any other star for that matter. That was her business– entertainment. "Yes. He sent me a response and told me to watch the interview." Laura pulled the phone away from her ear.

"Oh my AHHH!" Mandy screamed into the phone.

Laura laughed. "It's no big deal. I asked him in his letter to send me a smile."

"He also blew you a kiss." Reminded Mandy. "Have you talked to him, again?"

"He e-mailed me last night. We talked for a little bit back and forth." Admitted Laura.

"Oh my gosh!" exclaimed Mandy. "He likes you."

"He doesn't know me. Besides, I cut him off last night."

"What?" asked Mandy. "You cut him off? What does that mean?"

"I told him good night and got off of the computer before he could respond." Answered Laura, patiently.

"What? Why would you do that?"

"That is the last complication I need in my life right now. I already like him. I don't need to become infatuated with him."

"You don't like talking to him?" asked Mandy. "Are you sick? Do you have a fever?"

"No. Look, Mandy he's filming a movie right now and from what I understand, he's got another one after that. Then he has to travel and promote these movies. It's not like I'll ever meet him, anyway. Can we just let it go?"

There was silence on the other end of the line. "Mandy?" asked Laura.

"I'm here….Okay I'll let it go." Mandy answered, stiltedly.

Laura sighed. Now Mandy was going to pout because she was upset with her. "Good. How was your interview the other night?"

"Interesting. I talked to Stewart London. He just signed a record deal. He plays bluesy jazz type music. He's really good." Said Mandy. "I've heard him play in a couple of the clubs around here."

"I don't think I've heard of him." Responded Laura, racking her brain for anything that she might have heard about the musician.

"His single will be released next month, I think."

"I'll have to look for it."

"You do that." Answered Mandy, distractedly. "Well, I'd better go. Keep me updated, okay?"

Laura laughed. "If anything interesting happens in my life, you'll be the first to know."

"Okay. Great. Talk to you soon. Bye." Mandy practically sang into the phone and then hung up.

Laura smiled. Mandy was happy, again. Laura finished her salad and took her plate to the kitchen and washed the dishes. On her way back to the computer, she heard it beep, letting her know that she had new mail.

Laura sat down on the couch, grabbed her laptop off of the coffee table and opened her new message.

Laura,

An apology is not necessary but thank you. Keep yourself grounded? Hmm. That is an interesting way of putting it. I am on break before my next movie. I have two weeks off. I have plenty of time for other things. Want to chat? Do you have an IM?

Sebastian

Laura stared at his message for a minute and then googled Sebastian Thomas. She clicked on a link with pictures and studied them for a minute, glancing at his bio, noting that he was from London, hence the sexy accent. This was just too much. A popular actor didn't e-mail you and ask to talk on instant messenger. She minimized the pictures and went back to her e-mail. She typed a quick message.

L: How do I know that it's you? You might have someone read your mail and that's who I've been chatting with.

S: Someone else did not blow you a kiss on television, I did. Send me your IM name and I will find you when you log in. Mine is SebastianT20.

She typed her username quickly before she could have second thoughts.

L: Laura583

She logged into her IM service and waited. What was she doing? This was crazy. Was she really going to have a conversation with Sebastian Thomas? Well, an electronic conversation, anyway.

Her service beeped.

YOU HAVE A FRIEND REQUEST.

Laura clicked on it and sure enough, it was SebastianT20. She clicked accept.

S: Hello.

L: Hi.

S: Have a good day at work?

L: Yes.

S: Are we just going to play question and answer?

L: What do you want to talk about?

S: A question with a question.

L: (Laura rolled her eyes at his response.) What did you do all day?

S: Nothing.

L: You mean that literally, don't you?

S: Yes. But that is not entirely true. I worked out and read my script for my next film and checked out the message boards. Everyone sure is curious about the mysterious Laura.

L: That's your fault.

S: Yes. I know. My agent even asked me about you.

L: Oh?

S: Yes. I said I was having a secret affair and did not want to elaborate.

L: I'm sure that went over well.

S: He does not care. He just said that if it is so secret, I should not be saying your name on national television. I said I was so happy that I could not contain myself.

L: You did not.

S: LOL. No, but I thought about it.

L: What did you really say?

S: That it was a dedication to a special person.

Laura stared at the line that he had just typed. She could feel him reeling her in. This was definitely not a good idea.

S: Are you still there?

L: I'm here, but I should be going. I have to go to work early tomorrow.

S: Okay. I will not keep you from your rest. I will talk to you later.

L: Good night.

Laura signed off and got ready for bed. This was crazy. She had a crush on this guy, and she didn't even know him. Not really. And he **was** out of her league. What would a popular actor want with her? Just a normal woman. She wasn't anything special. She worked at a talent agency and saw people like him all the time. Most of them didn't look twice at her. She sighed and slid into bed. Most of the people she dealt with were stuck up, thinking that they were too good for everyone. Sebastian didn't seem like that.

- - - ❧ - - -

Sebastian signed off his instant messenger and started scanning the message boards. Everyone was curious about The Mysterious Laura. He smiled. Hmm. He was curious about her himself. He read through some of the blogs. <u>Has anyone found out who she is?</u>, <u>Has anyone seen Sebastian with her?</u>, <u>Does anyone know who Laura is?</u>, <u>Why haven't we seen her?</u>, <u>Do you think they've been together long?</u>

Sebastian read through several pages and then closed the links. It would be nice if his private life could stay private, but then he had better quit acting, huh? He shook his head. He enjoyed it too much. He would just not worry about the fan's thoughts on Laura. His cell phone rang, and he glanced at the caller id.

"Hello."

"Sebastian. Where are you hiding her?" his friend laughed over the line.

"Hello Jason. Hiding who?" Sebastian asked.

"Laura, of course. That is all I hear about."

"From whom?" asked Sebastian, curiously.

"Your fans of course."

"My fans?"

Jason laughed. "Yes. At my last interview. The interviewer asked if I had met Laura."

"Sorry about that, man."

"No big deal to me. I'm just curious when I get to meet her."

"There is no one to meet. We are just friends." Sebastian smiled to himself. That was kind of a stretch, but what was he going to say? Tell his friend that he did not even know who Laura was himself? Definitely not.

"No problem. Just introduce us when you're ready to share her with your friends." Jason laughed.

Sebastian started to argue and then caught himself. Just let Jason think what he wanted for now. Less questions to answer. "Aren't you too busy for socializing right now, anyway?"

"I'm never too busy for that." Answered Jason. "Be right there." He answered someone in the background. "I'll talk to you later. We're getting ready to shoot the next scene."

Sebastian hung up and leaned back in his chair. He had not really thought about how his comment would stir things up. Apparently, it was not only his fans that thought he had a secret girlfriend. His friends did, too.

Chapter Three

. . . .

*M*att handed three files to Laura. "Can you call these three and tell them about the photo shoot at the beach? If they aren't available, I've got a couple backups in mind, but these should do."

Laura nodded. "This shoot is just like the one two weeks ago, right?" Laura flipped open the top file.

"Yeah. They decided that they wanted two different groups." answered Matt over his shoulder, as he walked back to his office.

Laura reached for the phone and dialed the number.

"Hi, Jenny. This is Laura." She listened as the girl responded. "Yes, Matt has an assignment for you. A photo shoot on the beach this weekend. Just come by after three and pick up your voucher to fill out and get signed for confirmation of the job and instructions to take with you." Laura laughed, Jenny's excitement, contagious. "Okay. See you then."

She made two more calls and then went to Matt's office. "All good. They'll be by this afternoon to pick up their vouchers."

Matt nodded. "Thank you."

- - - ⌒ - - -

Laura hung up the phone as the lobby door opened.

"Hi, Laura." A guy walked up to the counter.

Laura glanced up at the tall blonde teenager in front of her. "Hello, Adam." Laura picked up an envelope from her desk and handed it to him. "Just bring this back to me by Wednesday."

Adam nodded. "You busy tonight?"

Laura tried not to smile. Adam asked her out every time he came by the agency. "Sorry, Adam. You know I don't date clients."

"I was hoping you had changed your mind." Adam watched her steadily with his green eyes.

Laura shook her head. "Sorry. Have fun this weekend. The shoot is at Tybee Island. Directions are in the envelope with the voucher."

Adam sighed. "Okay. Thanks. Have a good weekend." He turned and hurried out the door.

"You torture the poor boy." Commented Matt as he walked up to the counter.

Laura smiled at him. "He's only seventeen. He'll be fine."

Matt laughed. "You just break all of their hearts. How long do you think you can use the client line?"

"It's not a line. I don't date clients. Besides, I'm not interested in dating."

Matt studied her. "Yeah. You know, Donna asked me to get you to do the shoot this weekend."

Laura nodded. "She asked me about the shoot two weeks ago. I turned her down. I'm not interested."

"Don't you miss it at all?" asked Matt curiously. "You were very good at it. You still are when I can get you to fill in."

"No. Thank you, Matt, but I'm not changing my mind." She smiled at him. "Besides, what would you do without me to keep you straight?"

Matt laughed at her. "Yes, what would I do?" He winked and walked back to his office down the hall.

Laura let out a breath that she hadn't realized she was holding. Why was everyone so concerned about her career choice all of a sudden?

--- ❦ ---

"Mandy, I'm telling you, they are driving me crazy." Laura complained to her friend. She was lying on her bed with a pillow propped behind her head.

"I'm sure you are exaggerating." Said Mandy. "It can't be that bad."

"Donna, Lilly, Matt. They are all in on it."

Mandy laughed. "Laura. Do you want to model, again?"

"No." Laura responded immediately.

"Me thinks doth protest too quickly." Answered Mandy.

Laura sighed. "I'm not interested in doing that anymore."

"Okay. I was just asking. If you're not interested, then just ignore them and keep doing what you are doing. Besides, you're good at everything you do. Are you happy?"

"Yes."

"Then there's no problem."

Laura sighed. If only it were that easy.

--- ❦ ---

Laura stared at the screen in front of her. What was she doing? Not work. The page was blank. Her checkbook and budget were balanced in Quicken. She had updated all of her e-mail addresses. She had checked all of her e-mail and had deleted all of the garbage. She closed her word processing program and her IM screen popped up. SebastianT20 is on- line.

S: Hello.

L: Hi.

S: What are you doing up so late?

L: Nothing. (Laura pulled up Sebastian's picture and looked at it. Was she really talking to him? She studied the square jaw line and crooked nose, the blue eyes and disheveled hair.)

S: Nothing? So, you are just sitting there, staring at your computer?

L: (Laura laughed.) Actually, yes.

S: How is that working for you?

L: (She smiled) Well, you contacted me.

S: LOL. Is that good or bad?

L: I don't know. Are you trying to torture me or are you just bored?

S: I am not sure what you mean by that.

L: (Laura shook her head) Sorry. Bad day.

S: Oh. Want to talk about it?

L: No. How was your day?

S: Nice reversal there... Good.

L: What did you do?

S: I laid by the pool and did nothing.

L: No script reading?

S: No.

L: Working out in the gym?

S: No.

L: Hmm. So, you did do nothing.

S: Yes.

L: How did you like it?

S: I was bored.

L: LOL. Well, I guess I know you are not a lazy person.

S: No, I am not. I like to stay busy.

L: Me, too. What are you doing tomorrow?

S: I have an interview and then I'll probably go swimming.

L: Sounds like fun.

S: It is very invigorating.

L: The interview or swimming?

S: Ha! Ha! We are a comedian tonight. Swimming.

L: (Laura glanced at the clock). I didn't realize that it was so late. It's after two.

S: Yes. On a Saturday night, too???

L: No, I didn't have a date.

S: Why not?

L: Hmm. I don't have a boyfriend and I'm not interested in anyone.

S: So, it is not for lack of options, then.

L: LOL. I don't have men beating down my door to ask me out if that's what you mean. What about you? No date, either?

S: No. I do not have a girlfriend.

L: I'm sure there are plenty of girls happy about that and waiting in line to fill that position for you.

S: You mean for Simon.

L: Some of them, but some of them are for you.

An hour later, Laura yawned and glanced at her bed.

L: I think I'd better go before I fall asleep on you.

S: Yes. Same here. Goodnight.

L: Goodnight.

Laura climbed into bed smiling. It had been nice chatting with Sebastian. It actually seemed kind of normal if she didn't think about the fact that he was an up-and-coming star.

--- ✑ ---

"So, while I am out on one of the worst dates of my life, you are at home chatting on-line with Sebastian Thomas?" asked Mandy, incredulously.

Laura smiled. "If that was Saturday night, then yes."

"What has changed since the last time we spoke about him?"

"Nothing."

"Nothing? You're talking to the guy and it's nothing?" exclaimed Mandy.

Laura rolled her eyes. "We are just talking. It's not like we're having a secret affair."

"You could."

Laura laughed out loud. "I'm sorry. I thought I just heard you say to have an affair with Sebastian Thomas."

"I did." Responded Mandy.

"Tell me about this date." Insisted Laura, changing the subject.

"It was the worst date that I have ever had in my life." Complained Mandy. "I met the guy- his name was Brad. I met him at the restaurant. It was a nice restaurant. You know with linen napkins and China. He had the worst manners. It was embarrassing. He slurped his soup."

Laura tried to stifle a laugh, but it slipped out.

"It's not funny." Mandy tried to sound mad but ruined it by laughing. "Okay, it's funny now, but at the time, I was horrified. He had a bowl of soup and then ordered a burger and loaded it with ketchup and mustard and had ketchup dribbling down his chin. He finished his soda and sucked every single drop out of the cup. You know how it is when you get to the bottom of the cup. It's so loud. People were staring at us. The waiter was even sending me sympathetic looks." Mandy sighed. "I was so glad that I hadn't let him pick me up. He even said he would call me."

"What did you tell him?" asked Laura, trying to catch her breath from laughing so hard.

"I didn't say anything. I left as fast as I could."

Laura grabbed a tissue and dabbed at her eyes. She was laughing so hard, she had tears streaming down her face. "Has he called you?"

"No. I hope he doesn't, but just in case, I'm screening my calls." Answered Mandy.

"Where did you meet this guy?"

"He was at one of our photo shoots. He was cute and seemed intelligent, but I can't handle the lack of manners."

"He's not someone that you'll see often, is he?" asked Laura.

"No. Thank goodness. He was just a temp runner for the photographer."

"Well, that's good."

"Don't think I forgot what we were talking about." Reminded Mandy.

Laura sighed. "Sebastian and I are just talking on-line. It's no big deal."

"You can say that all you want, but the fact that he is spending time talking to you is a big deal. He must like you." Insisted Mandy.

"We just like talking to each other. That's all." Clarified Laura.

Mandy laughed sarcastically. "Okay. I give up." She sighed. "It's too hard to corrupt you from here."

Laura laughed. "You finally admit it. My bad habits are all your fault."

"Oh no. You can't blame that on me. If that was the case, you'd have some fun bad habits."

"I have plenty of **fun** bad habits." Laura answered, huffily.

Mandy laughed. "Don't get upset. I didn't mean that you aren't fun. You just don't have enough fun."

Laura sighed. "You're probably right about that, but I have too much other stuff to do."

"That's my point." Mandy responded. "You need to make more time for yourself."

Laura didn't respond. She knew her friend was right but that just didn't fit into her schedule.

- - -⦵- - -

Laura's week seemed to creep by, but she knew things would pick up later in the week. She had stacks of resumes for various crew positions and movie roles to back up that theory.

She had just sat back down at her desk, when the lobby door opened, and a tall blonde-haired man stepped into the lobby. She smiled at him. "Hi. May I help you?"

"Yes. I'm Luke Peters. I have a two o'clock appointment with Matt Logan." He answered

Laura nodded. "Right. For the Key Grip position. Have a seat and I'll let Matt know that you're here."

"Thank you." Luke walked over to one of the chairs and sat down while Laura walked back to Matt's office.

Laura tapped on the door and then stepped in when Matt looked up. "Luke Peters is here."

Matt nodded. "Okay. I'll be right with him."

Laura went back out to her desk and glanced at Luke. "He'll be with you in a few minutes." She sat down and pulled up her calendar on the computer to double check the appointments for the rest of the day. So far, Tuesday had progressed slowly, but they had back-to-back interviews with technical crew for the rest of the day and Wednesday and Thursday. Things would only get busier from there.

- - -⦵- - -

Laura stared at her Instant Messenger login screen. She had been thinking about Sebastian all day. All day every day for the last week if she was honest with herself. This was exactly what she had been trying to avoid. Infatuation with someone who was unattainable.

What was she doing? They had talked several times over the last week and she had really enjoyed herself. He seemed really down to earth and was easy to chat with. Of course, they were on-line. Not looking into those sexy blue eyes probably kept her from being tongue tied. She signed in and looked at her friends list. He wasn't on-line. She sighed. That was probably for the best, anyway. She was just getting deeper and deeper into a situation that she didn't want. Her computer beeped. *SebastianT20 is on-line.* She laughed. Right. She didn't want to talk to Sebastian. She could tell everyone else that, but she couldn't lie to herself.

L: Hi, Sebastian.

S: Hello.

L: How have you been?

S: Good. Busy doing interviews and promotions for *Royalty Unknown.* How are you?

L: Good. I was just getting ready for bed.

S: I just caught you then, huh?

L: (Laura smiled). Yes. Were you looking for me for a reason?

S: Just to say hi.

L: So, do you have a lot more promoting to do?

S: Actually, no. I have a week to do whatever I want and then we start filming my next movie.

L: Better enjoy your week off then.

S: Yes, I will.

L: I'd better run. I've got a busy day tomorrow.

S: Okay. Good night.

L: Good night.

Laura signed off and shut down her computer. She smiled to herself as she got ready for bed. That was an interesting conversation.

He was thinking about her, too. She climbed into bed and snuggled into the covers. Sleep. She told herself. No dreaming about Sebastian. She closed her eyes and fell asleep with Sebastian's image in her mind.

- - -◈- - -

Laura answered the phone and signed for a package, then waved at the delivery guy as he left. "No, Monica. Matt is not seeing anyone today. All of the auditions are tomorrow."

"I want to speak to him." Monica demanded.

"I can give him a message. He's in a meeting right now and will be for most of the day."

"You're just saying that."

"No, I'm not. He is in a meeting and I have people in front of me that I need to take care of. Do you want me to give him a message?"

Monica sighed into the phone. "No. I'll see him tomorrow. Just tell him I'll be there."

"I will. Thank you. Goodbye." She hung up the phone and looked up to find Lance standing in front of her.

"Is Monica in the pile?" he asked.

"No. Matt didn't think she would be right for the part."

Matt walked up. "Who?"

"Monica." Laura answered. "She said to tell you that she would be here tomorrow."

"She isn't right for the part. She will just be wasting everyone's time." He shook his head. "Some of my clients drive me crazy. They think they know more than me."

Laura glanced at her desk. "Do you want your messages?"

"Anything priority?" asked Matt.

"Not really. Lilly called about a couple of perfume models and Clay needs a couple of pirates for a commercial next week. I think they could be handled on Monday."

"You have any ideas for those?"

Laura nodded. "Yes."

Matt glanced at the clock. "It's already 6:00."

"I'll be here until 7:00. I know tomorrow's a big day."

"I think we've got everything set for tomorrow. If you're going to stay, why don't you pull the files of who you think can handle the jobs and put them on my desk? I'll take a look at them and let you know what I think about your choices."

"Matt, I'm not the agent. I'm not qualified." Protested Laura.

Matt laughed. "You've been working here for five years. You've ran this office, modeled, taken pictures, filled in for actresses, set up casting calls, found locations, need I go on?"

Laura's eyes widened. He remembered all of that?

"That doesn't make me qualified."

"That makes you an office manager/agent assistant, model, photographer, actress, etc. You're plenty qualified and if I ever decide that I want a partner, you'll be the first one I ask. You're practically a partner anyway." Matt explained.

Lance smiled. "And I'm a witness to that. If he ever tries to deny what he just said, just let me know."

"Matt. Thank you." Laura smiled. It was nice to be appreciated. It also helped that she enjoyed her job, so she loved being in the middle of everything. She could be in the middle, but also on the sidelines.

He smiled at her. "You're welcome. Now, get finished up, so you can get out of here."

Lance winked at her as he followed Matt into the conference room.

- - - ❦ - - -

Laura pulled the files and put them on Matt's desk, then set up the lobby for the next morning. After double checking everything, she gathered her things and went home. She took a shower and ate a quick dinner and then sat down with her laptop on the couch. She glanced at the IM icon and then shrugged. Why not? She signed in and then checked her e-mail. The IM screen beeped and then popped up on her screen.

S: Hello.

L: (She smiled) Hi.

S: How was work?

L: Long.

S: Did you just get home?

L: Yes. Work is crazy right now.

S: We have never talked about your job. What do you do?

L: I'm an office manager.

S: And you work this late?

L: I work for *Studio B.*

S: You work for Matt Logan?

L: Yes. (Laura frowned) Do you know him?

S: I have done some work with him. He trades off with my agent sometimes.

L: Walter Robertson.

S: Yes.

L: I should have figured that out.

S: Small world. How long have you been working for Matt?

L: Five years.

S: I bet I have seen you before.

L: I'm sure I'd remember if you'd been in the office.

S: Not in person. I have heard about his famous assistant, though.

L: LOL. Famous, huh?

S: He says you do everything.

L: I'm not Superwoman.

S: The way Matt talks about you, you are.

L: What I do is no big deal. Anyone could do it.

S: I think that you are being modest.

L: I enjoy my job.

S: That definitely helps.

L: So, what did you do today?

S: Script work and gym. Some swimming.

L: Busy day.

S: Apparently not as busy as yours.

L: Tomorrow will be worse.

S: You are working on Saturday?

L: Casting call.

S: I see.

L: So, are you hiding out? I read on the message boards that no one
knows where you are.

S: Yes. I read that, too. They think I am with the Mysterious Laura.

L: That's me. Mysterious.

S: You will not let me meet you.

L: I don't have time for a personal life right now.

S: Why not?

L: After the casting call, we'll be super busy setting everything up for
the filming and then the actual filming and editing and well,
you know what all it entails.

S: Yes, but you do not have to do all of it.

L: No, but I'll be busy with whatever Matt needs.

S: No wonder he talks so highly of you.

L: I'm not sure that was a compliment.

S: I was not being insulting. I just think you overwork yourself.

 L: Maybe. Sometimes it doesn't feel like work, though.

S: I know what you mean.

L: I believe you do.

S: Well, I guess I had better let you go, huh? What time do you have
    to be in tomorrow?

L: 8:00.

S: I'll talk to you later then.

L: Goodnight.

S: Goodnight.

Laura smiled as she signed off. She felt her feet lifting off the
ground. She stomped them as she got up and brushed her teeth before
getting into bed. Exactly what she was trying to avoid. She didn't
have time for her head to be in the clouds. No daydreaming allowed.

Sebastian stared at the computer screen for a minute and then
smiled to himself. He glanced at his watch. Yeah, it could work.
He picked up the phone and started making calls, then grabbed his
duffel and started packing his clothes. With any luck, he could leave
within the hour.

Chapter Four

The next day was too busy for any thoughts of Sebastian as the agency lobby filled up with people auditioning for *Dawn's Cover*. Between that and collecting faxes of technical applications for the filming crew, Laura and Elizabeth, Matt's girlfriend, stayed steadily busy all morning. Laura appreciated Elizabeth's help. Elizabeth tried to come in and help when the office was really busy. Matt and Elizabeth had been together for as long as Laura could remember, so Elizabeth knew how busy things would get when they started filming.

"Laura, can you read with Damon?" asked Elizabeth. "I'll watch the desk for you."

Laura glanced up from her papers, at the tall, lithe blonde. "Sure. Where is he?"

"In the storage room." Elizabeth shrugged. "It's the only place that he could find privacy."

Laura laughed. "I know he hates to run through the script with people in the room." She handed the list to Elizabeth. "How'd you get roped into this?"

"It's the only way I could see Matt." Elizabeth sighed. "We are going out to dinner later."

"Good. I keep telling him not to work so hard."

"I appreciate everything that you do. If it wasn't for you, I'd never see him." Said Elizabeth.

"Thank you, Elizabeth." They both glanced at the conference room door as a woman stepped out. Laura pointed at the list. "I think Tara is next."

"I got it. Go help Damon. He's up soon."

"Okay." Laura grabbed her copy of the script off her desk and walked down the hall to the storage room. She tapped on the door. "Damon, its Laura."

The door opened and she was pulled inside. "Shh. They'll hear you." He whispered, glancing around.

Laura sighed. Damon was already into character and she knew exactly where he was. She leaned against the other wall and glanced at her script. *"We lost them. They couldn't have found us so soon."*

"They're fast. They can't be more than minutes behind us. Be quiet."

Laura watched as he peeked behind some boxes, watching something intently. Then he turned and walked over to her. "They passed us." He grabbed her hand and pulled her close. "I don't know what I'd do if something happened to you. I've got to get you out of here."

"I'm not leaving without you."

"I'll be fine as long as you're safe."

"I won't leave you." Laura put her hand on his cheek and looked into his eyes. "I can't leave you to fight them alone."

"You have to. I'll be too distracted if I'm worrying about you."

Damon leaned towards her and Laura put her fingers over his lips to stop him. "That was great, Damon. I think they're calling you."

"Laura. You never let me have any fun." whined Damon.

Laura smiled. "This is an audition, remember? Stay focused."

"I was." Damon teased as they left the storage room.

"Laura, Matt wants you to go in with Damon." Said Elizabeth as Laura and Damon reached the lobby.

"Okay. Thanks Elizabeth." Laura followed Damon into the conference room, and they stood quietly against the wall. Matt and Lance were listening to two people read.

"Thank you very much." Said Matt as the two finished their audition and left the room. He jotted down some notes and then glanced at Laura. "Would you mind reading with the next few guys?"

"No. I don't mind." Answered Laura. Matt was looking at her strangely.

She raised an eyebrow at him, and he nodded towards Damon. "Whenever you're ready." Said Matt.

Laura turned to Damon. "Same scene?"

Damon nodded and smiled. Laura rolled her eyes at him, knowing exactly what he was thinking. He might be talented and handsome, but he wasn't her type.

- - - ℰℑ - - -

Several hours later, Laura sat in a chair with her feet propped up, listening to Matt and Lance talk. The auditions were over, and they were discussing casting possibilities.

"I definitely like Damon." Said Lance.

Matt nodded. "He's very talented. He'll be great for the role of Garrett."

"What about Kylee?" asked Lance.

"Who do you think matched the character that you wrote the best?" asked Matt.

"Tara was good." Said Lance. "What did you think, Laura?"

"I think you're right. Tara and Damon were the best." Answered Laura, glancing at the audition tape playing in front of them.

"Although, this girl isn't bad. I think her name was Emma." She glanced at the names list on the table.

There was a tap on the door and then Elizabeth opened the door and poked her head in. "Laura, there's a delivery for you."

Laura sat up and dropped her feet to the floor. "For me?"

"Why don't you lock the front door, Laura and then the four of us can relax while we look over the rest of the auditions?" suggested Matt.

Laura nodded in agreement as she walked over to the door. "I'll lock up. Elizabeth, go have a seat and relax. Thank you for your help."

Elizabeth smiled and followed Laura into the lobby.

Laura stopped and frowned. "Did Matt send you flowers?" she glanced at the delivery guy standing in the doorway, whose face was blocked by the flowers.

"No. He said the delivery was for you." Answered Elizabeth. She walked over to the flowers and plucked the card from amongst the lilies, then handed it to Laura.

Laura accepted the card and pulled it out of the envelope. "Why would anyone send me flowers?" she opened the card.

Join me for dinner?

Laura glanced up at the flowers, questioningly.

"You do like lilies, don't you?" asked Sebastian as he lowered the bouquet of flowers and smiled at her.

Laura stepped back. "Sebastian?" she glanced at the bouquet of purple lilies in his hands. "What are you doing here?"

Elizabeth laughed. "That's obvious. He came to take you out to dinner."

Laura glanced from Elizabeth to Sebastian. "How did you know that I like lilies?" She knew she sounded like an idiot, but she couldn't stop herself from blurting it out.

"I told him." Answered Elizabeth looking at Laura curiously. "It was actually kind of interesting. He called this morning and told me who he was and what he wanted to do." She glanced over at Sebastian. "Of course, I wasn't sure that it was really him or that I should answer any questions about you, so I had Matt talk to him. He explained everything to Matt and well, here he is."

"It was really you." Gasped Laura. Another stupid remark, she thought.

"I told you it was." Answered Sebastian.

"I just didn't know why you would talk to me." Said Laura. "There are plenty of women out there that are in your circle."

"They are not you." Answered Sebastian, sincerely.

Laura stared at Sebastian for a moment, taking him in. It just didn't seem real for him to be standing right in front of her. She glanced over his clothes. He was wearing black dress slacks and a beige button-down shirt with a black sport coat and black dress shoes. The sport coat emphasized his broad shoulders and the shirt pulled tautly over his muscular chest. His blue eyes were accented by the dark colors.

"I don't have anything to wear." She said.

"I took care of that." Said Elizabeth. "There's a dress for you in Matt's office."

Laura glanced at Elizabeth in surprise. "Oh. Thank you." She glanced around; noticing Matt and Lance had joined them. She glanced shyly at Sebastian. "Excuse me." Laura rushed down the hall to Matt's office and shut the door. Then she leaned against it, took a deep breath and pinched herself. *Ow!* She rubbed her arm. Yes. She was awake. She stepped away from the door and glanced around Matt's office.

A moment later, there was a tap on the door and then Elizabeth stepped into the room. "I thought you might need your purse."

Laura turned to Elizabeth. "He's really here for me?"

Elizabeth nodded. "Yes. He seems to be really interested in you. He was asking me all kinds of questions. It almost seemed like he was nervous."

"To see me?" asked Laura incredulously. She couldn't believe that Sebastian Thomas was there to take her to dinner. Her. Laura Steele. Just a normal woman. Nobody special. She glanced at herself in the mirror beside the door. She looked so plain. And he was so handsome!

Elizabeth put her hand on Laura's arm. "You're the only one who doesn't think you're great. Matt talks highly of you all of the time."

"He exaggerates." Insisted Laura.

Elizabeth shook her head. "No. He doesn't. I've been around long enough. I see how you work. You can tell you enjoy your job. You always help out with whatever you can. You solve almost any problem that comes up. Besides that, I've been with Matt for several years and I know him, and he does not give praise unless it's earned."

"Matt's so lucky to have you." Responded Laura.

Elizabeth laughed. "Enough of this. You have a date. Get dressed. I'll wait here." She pushed Laura towards the bathroom adjoining Matt's office.

--- ❧ ---

Sebastian looked at Matt and Lance. "That didn't go very well."

"She'll be fine. Just give her a few minutes." Said Matt.

Sebastian glanced around at the pictures on the wall. "Is this Laura?" he studied a picture of her lounging on a large rock on the beach. She was wearing a dark green one-piece bathing suit with sunglasses and a floppy hat.

"Yes. It's the only picture she'll let me display." Answered Matt. "She's very self-conscious. She's talented, but you can't convince her of that."

"I got that impression talking to her on-line." Said Sebastian. He smiled at Matt. "We will see what I can do to change that."

"What are your intentions?" asked Matt, his brow arched curiously.

"I just want to get to know her." Answered Sebastian. "Spend time with her. I thought I might take her to the premiere of *Midnight Bayou.*"

"I'm not sure if that's a good idea. As soon as she's seen with you, her life is no longer private. Don't put her in that position unless you're sure that you want to be with her."

Sebastian nodded. "Fair enough."

"Just be good to her or you'll have to answer to me." Advised Matt.

Sebastian smiled at Matt. "I thought you were okay with this."

"I am okay with you two going out on a date. We'll see about the rest."

Sebastian laughed. "Okay. We'll see about the rest."

Elizabeth came down the hall and stopped next to Matt. "She'll be out in a minute." She told Sebastian and then turned to Matt. "Are you about ready to go?"

"I need to finish looking over the tapes." He answered. "There are a couple people to call back, I think."

Laura walked down the hallway in a burgundy velvet dress with spaghetti straps and lace trim. She had a black lace shawl across her shoulders and wore black strappy high heels. Her auburn hair hung loosely to her shoulders and the only jewelry she wore was her birthstone necklace. "You always say that. I think it's time to leave for the day." She commented as she stopped next to them in the lobby.

Matt smiled at her. "Soon." He glanced at Sebastian. "So, you two are going to *Little Italy*. I've already spoken to Papa Moretti and he's expecting you. Use the side door and you should be able to get in unnoticed. He's got a private room set up for you."

"Thank you, Matt." Said Laura. "Shall we take my car?"

Matt shook his head. "No. Take mine. That's what Sebastian's driving anyway. I've got all my windows tinted. You've only got your back windows tinted. That way, you'll have less of a chance of getting noticed while driving around town."

Laura nodded. "Okay. Apparently, you all have been busy plotting." She turned to Sebastian. "Thank you for the flowers." He handed them to her. "I didn't mean to leave you holding them."

"No problem." Responded Sebastian.

"You two should get going." Matt instructed.

"I need to get my bag." Said Laura.

Matt shook his head. "No. There's no working over the rest of the weekend. Everything can wait until Monday."

"Then you should be leaving, too." Remarked Laura.

"We will be leaving in an hour. Elizabeth and I have plans for tomorrow. We're spending the whole day out of town."

"Oh?" Laura arched her brow in question at Matt. "Great. I'll see you later then." She turned to Elizabeth. "Thank you for everything."

Elizabeth smiled. "You are very welcome. Have a good time."

- - - ∞ - - -

Laura and Sebastian walked out to the car and drove the five blocks to the restaurant. They pulled into a parking space on the left side of the building and parked. Sebastian got out and walked around to Laura's door. She had the door open and was stepping out of the car, so he offered her his arm and closed the door for her.

She smiled at him. "Thank you." She nodded to the left. "The entrance is that way."

They crossed the parking lot to the stone pathway and kept their faces averted from the crowd in hopes that no one would recognize Sebastian. When they reached the door, Sebastian held it open for Laura and then entered behind her. There was someone waiting for them just inside the door. "Hello, Laura." Raoul smiled at them. "Welcome."

"Hi, Raoul. This is Sebastian. Sebastian, this is Raoul. His family owns the restaurant." Laura watched the two as they shook hands. Sebastian treated Raoul like an old friend. Not stuck up at all.

"Nice to meet you, Raoul. Thank you for accommodating us." Said Sebastian, appreciatively.

"No problem." Raoul glanced from Sebastian to Laura. "Follow me, please." They crossed the hall and entered a door to the private dining rooms in the back. "We set up a table for you by the fireplace. I didn't think you'd want to sit near the window, so I drew the drapes."

"Thank you very much, Raoul. I'm sorry to put you to so much trouble." Said Laura, apologetically.

Raoul laughed. "No trouble at all. You know we'd do anything for you, Laura. You're practically family."

"I'm addicted to the food." She glanced at Sebastian. "Unfortunately for my figure, I eat here at least once a week."

Sebastian's gaze softly traced over her. "I don't see anything wrong with your figure." He pulled her chair out for her.

Laura sat down. "Thank you. I wasn't fishing for a compliment."

Sebastian sat in the chair across from her. "I know."

"May I get you something to drink?" asked Raoul. He turned to Sebastian and handed him the wine list.

Sebastian glanced over the wine list as Raoul handed them each a menu.

"I'll just have water for now, please." Answered Laura.

"That will be fine for me, too." Answered Sebastian. He watched Raoul leave and then turned back to Laura. "Back to the conversation. You look beautiful."

Laura smiled, letting her eyes appraise him, slowly, before returning back to his face. "Thank you. You're quite handsome yourself."

He raised an eyebrow. "Thank you. I am impressed you accepted a compliment."

"I can do that occasionally." She glanced at her menu, then back at Sebastian. "Are you hungry?"

"Starving." Answered Sebastian, his eyes never leaving her face.

Laura felt a shiver run up her spine and tore her eyes away from his penetrating blue ones. She looked at the menu, thankful that she had been there before because she had no idea what she was reading.

Raoul returned with a pitcher of water and a basket of bread sticks. He filled their water glasses. "Are you ready to order?" he asked.

Laura nodded. "You know me. I've got to have Mama's manicotti and a side salad with house dressing."

Raoul nodded and then turned to Sebastian. "What would you like, sir?"

"I will have the shrimp linguine and a Caesar salad." Answered Sebastian.

"Very good. I'll put your orders in. Is there anything else that I can get you while you wait?"

Sebastian glanced at Laura. "Would you like a glass of wine?"

Laura nodded. "Yes, thank you. With my salad will be fine."

Sebastian turned to Raoul. "She'll have a glass of Chianti and I'll have a glass of Cabernet Sauvignon."

Raoul smiled. "Yes, sir." He left the room, carefully shutting the door behind him.

"So, how did you manage all of this so quickly?" asked Laura.

Sebastian's mouth tilted up into a one-sided smile. "You underestimate me. I told you that I wanted to meet you. You told me where you worked. After that, it was easy."

"Yes, but you're not staying in Savannah, are you? No, I would have heard, I'm sure."

"No, I am not staying in Savannah." Sebastian answered, a smile on his lips, his eyes twinkling with amusement from her answering her own question.

"Where are you staying?" asked Laura, she leaned towards him. "Do I get to know your secret hideaway?"

Sebastian laughed. "I was staying in a beach house in Malibu."

"Ahh. Right under everyone's noses. That's the best place to hide."

"Yes."

"I talked to you last night in Malibu, right?" asked Laura.

"Yes. I decided last night to come and see you. I was coming this way anyway. We will be filming in Hilton Head, so I just came early. Matt had his car at the airport for me and I drove straight to the studio."

"Where'd you get the flowers?" asked Laura.

"I saw a little flower shop on the way and stopped. There was an older woman behind the counter. She did not seem to recognize me. I paid with cash." Answered Sebastian.

"Hmm. Between the airport and here. I'd say that was Molly's." she smiled at him. "You picked the best place. Molly doesn't gossip. She stays out of other people's business."

Sebastian nodded in agreement. "She did not ask a lot of questions. Just gave me what I asked for and let me pick out a card."

"I love the lilies. Thank you. They are my favorite flower." Laura gazed into his blue eyes. She heard the door open and pulled her gaze away from his, then glanced at her watch. "I hope Matt is not still at the studio."

Raoul set the salads in front of them. "Fresh ground pepper?" he sprinkled some on each of their salads after their nods of assent and excused himself after setting their wine glasses on the table.

"Speaking of Matt. What was that look about at the studio?" asked Sebastian, curiously.

Laura smiled. "Oh, you noticed that, huh?"

"Yes."

"Well, Matt bought an engagement ring for Elizabeth. He showed it to me last week. I'm hoping that means that he's going to propose to her tomorrow. He told me that he was going to wait until the movie was finished, but that will take months and I don't think he should put it off."

"And you told him that?"

"Yes. Why put it off? If he knows that he loves her and wants to be with her, then go ahead and ask her to marry him. Life is too unpredictable to not do things when you have the opportunity." Laura glanced down at her salad. She seemed to be running her mouth a little tonight. Hmm. It was very easy to be herself around him. That was something she hadn't anticipated. She took a bite of her salad and glanced up. Sebastian was watching her.

"What?" she asked after she had finished chewing and had swallowed her food.

"Do not get shy now. I like it when you tell me what is on your mind." Sebastian answered.

"I'm not being shy. I'm eating. You said yourself that you were starving." Laura stuck another forkful of salad in her mouth and chewed slowly. There. Her pulse was slowing down a little. It was very easy to talk to him just like a regular person. But he's not a regular person, she told herself as she finished eating her salad. He's the new heartthrob and all the teenage girls and some adult women would do anything to be sitting where she was at the moment. She pushed her plate to the side and glanced up at Sebastian who was still watching her, but also eating his salad.

"Why do you look at me like that?" she asked curiously, as she took a bread stick from the basket in the center of the table.

"I like watching you. After all, the way you talk, I will probably never get to see you, again with your busy lifestyle and all."

"Don't you get that attitude with me, mister." She pointed her breadstick at him.

Sebastian laughed and leaned over and took a bite of the breadstick. "Mmm. Thank you."

Laura started laughing. "You so ruined my sternness."

--- ❦ ---

Raoul put their bag of leftovers on the chair next to the table. "Here you go."

Laura eyed the bag. "We didn't have that many leftovers."

"I know. Mama wanted to send you some dessert and some extra manicotti."

Laura grabbed her purse. "At least let me pay for it." Raoul looked taken aback. "You would offend Mama."

Laura smiled. "Okay. Thank you, Raoul. Thank Mama for me, too."

Sebastian passed the folder with the ticket and money in it to Raoul.

"Thank you, Raoul. Please, tell Mama everything was delicious."

Raoul nodded. "Thank you. I will."

Sebastian stood up and Laura followed. She picked up the bag from the chair and they followed Raoul to the door.

Raoul peeked out. "Everything's clear, but things are busy out front, so be careful." He cautioned.

Laura nodded. "Thank you." She and Sebastian slipped out the door, across the hall and out of the restaurant unnoticed.

They made it to the car without any incidents. "Where to, now?" asked Sebastian as he held the passenger door open for Laura. He closed it after she climbed inside and got settled, then walked around to the driver's side.

Laura glanced at Sebastian as he slid into the driver's seat. "Well, we can't go anywhere public unless we want to be mobbed, so I guess my place." She glanced around as they backed out of the parking spot. "Turn left out of the lot and drive two blocks then turn right. We'll follow that road several blocks before we reach my place."

Sebastian nodded and followed her directions.

Twenty minutes later, they pulled into a parking spot in front of her apartment building and got out of the car. Laura grabbed the bag of food and her flowers from the back seat. Sebastian took the bag from Laura and motioned for her to precede him. They made it into her apartment and Laura laughed delightedly. "I kept expecting someone to notice you."

"I tried to be really careful coming here. I didn't want to put you on the spot like that."

"I appreciate that." Laura answered as she walked towards the kitchen. She pulled a vase out of a cabinet and filled it with water, then began trimming the stems of the flowers and placing them into the vase.

"Would you like for me to put this in the refrigerator?" asked Sebastian, as he set the bag on the counter and glanced inside.

"Yes. Thank you." Answered Laura as she arranged the flowers in the vase.

Sebastian took the containers out of the bag and placed them in the refrigerator, then turned his attention to Laura. He let his gaze slide over her face and the creamy skin of her shoulders, her deep auburn hair. She was breathtaking and she didn't even realize it.

Laura placed the last flower in the vase and carried them to the living room. She placed them on the coffee table and turned to Sebastian. "Can I get you a glass of wine? I have a bottle of Chardonnay."

"Yes. That would be fine." He answered. He watched her get the glasses out of the cabinet and pull a bottle of wine from her wine rack in the kitchen. She pulled a corkscrew out of a drawer and he stepped forward. "May I?"

She handed it to him. "Of course. Thank you." She watched as he popped the cork and poured the wine into the glasses.

He picked up the glasses and gestured towards the living room. "Ladies first." He followed her into the living room.

"May I?" Sebastian nodded toward the couch.

"Of course. I'm sorry. That was rude of me." Laura sat across from him in her favorite comfy chair. "I had a great time tonight."

"I did, too." He handed her one of the glasses. "So, you are not mad at me?" he asked sheepishly.

Laura laughed. "As if I could be mad at you."

Sebastian shrugged. "I was not sure. I just knew that I wanted to meet you in person."

"Well, I'm glad you did." Her gaze traveled slowly over him, stopping briefly at the top two buttons of his shirt that were casually left unbuttoned. "What girl could complain about you going through all this trouble to see her?"

"I told you. I am a person like everyone else."

"Yes. You are, but you're also more." She looked into his deep blue eyes. "You're very talented. You become the characters that you portray on screen. You touch people's lives with your acting. You are quickly becoming the hottest new star."

"I enjoy acting and I want to continue to do that, but I also would like to see you. I would like to get to know you."

"Is that something that you're willing to do privately? I'm not ready to have the world watching my every move." Responded Laura, wondering where her boldness was coming from. A famous star says he wants to get to know you and you tell him you don't want anyone to know about it. Smart.

"I can handle that for now. I know you will be busy here filming this movie. I will be filming another movie in a few days. I will be tied up with that for a while." He sighed. "There is a good bit of travel involved with this next movie, too. We have some promoting and interviews to do for it."

Laura nodded. "I understand that. I'm sure you'll be busy for quite a while."

"We can talk a lot."

"Sure. And text message. Instant messenger has worked well." Answered Laura. "We'll see how things go."

"Okay." Agreed Sebastian. "We will see how things go."

"I think, though, that at some point you're going to want someone on your arm at these events." Commented Laura.

"You." Responded Sebastian. He patted the couch beside him. "You can sit over here. I will not bite you."

Laura smiled and stood up, then moved to the end of the couch. She slid off her shoes and folded her legs under her, then turned towards him. "So, tell me Mr. Thomas. Do you have any deep, dark secrets?" She took a drink of her wine and then set the glass on the coffee table.

Sebastian smiled his crooked smile. "Hmm I like red heads."

Laura pulled her shawl tighter around her shoulders.

"Are you cold?" Sebastian removed his coat and placed it around her shoulders, then grabbed the afghan off the back of the couch and draped it across her lap.

"Better. Thank you." Laura turned her head slightly and inhaled the smell of his jacket. It had a kind of spicy scent. Maybe his after shave. She snuggled into the warmth of his jacket. "Well?"

Sebastian shook his head. "Nothing I can think of. You?"

Laura laughed softly. "Yeah, I do." She leaned towards him and whispered. "I have the world's biggest heartthrob in my living room." She stared into his eyes and watched as he leaned closer to her, then her eyelids fluttered closed.

"When we return, we will answer some letters from the mail bag." The television blared to life and they jumped apart.

Laura laughed as she leaned back and pulled the remote from between the cushions. She set it on the coffee table and leaned back against the arm of the couch. "Shall we listen to the letters from the mail bag?"

Sebastian smiled. "Curious about the stars, are we?"

"I watch the show occasionally to keep up on upcoming movies and such. Sometimes, there's even some good gossip." Laura smiled mischievously.

"Oh, yeah?" asked Sebastian. "Like what?"

"Shh." Said Laura as she returned her attention to the television.

"A few nights ago, we interviewed Sebastian Thomas, and everyone is wondering who Laura is. Honestly, gals, he didn't tell me anything. We have heard, though, that there is a Laura starring with him in his next movie. The filming for 'Worlds Apart' will start early June. The only information we have about this movie is that it is a science fiction movie with action and romance that happens on Earth and not in outer space. We'll let you know when we know more." Marla reached for another letter and Laura hit mute on the remote.

"A science fiction romance, huh? Sounds like I'm off the hook." Said Laura. "Is she your romantic interest in the movie?"

Sebastian shook his head. "No. She is my sister in the movie."

"Ooh. That's some juicy gossip that you've started now." Teased Laura.

"There is always gossip about someone. I am sure all will be fine. They will find someone else to talk about soon." He regarded Laura. "Seriously, though, I have known Laura for a while and there is nothing romantic there."

"Okay. You certainly don't have to explain anything to me." Answered Laura.

Sebastian sighed in exasperation. "Any other deep, dark secrets you have?"

Laura smiled and glanced at the clock. "I turn into a pumpkin at midnight."

"That is why you always rushed off of the computer." Said Sebastian. "And here I thought it was me."

"No, you didn't." Argued Laura, looking into his eyes intently. Surely, he was joking. He wouldn't think that **she** didn't like **him**.

She should be the one wondering why he was here. Someone as handsome and talented and even personable with someone plain and ordinary like her.

"Do not even go there." Sebastian frowned at her. "What?" asked Laura in surprise.

"I see what you are thinking. It is all over your face. You **are** someone that I feel is worth getting to know." He held her gaze. "Now, tell me about yourself."

Laura giggled. "Are you trying to intimidate me into talking?"

"Is it working?" asked Sebastian.

Laura shook her head. "No. I'll make a deal with you. You ask a question; I ask a question."

Sebastian thought about it for a minute and then shook his head. "Not fair. You probably already know way more about me."

"Like what?" asked Laura innocently.

"Like whatever you hear on-line, on television, in magazines. My life is an open book."

"Okay. Two for one. That's my final offer."

"Deal." Agreed Sebastian.

Chapter Five

"This cake is delicious." Said Sebastian as he put a bite of the cake into his mouth.

Laura nodded and closed her eyes. "It is my favorite." She savored the light homemade butter cake covered in fruit and layered with fruit filling. She opened her eyes to find Sebastian watching her with a burning intensity in his eyes. Her breath caught and she felt like she would melt into a puddle on the couch. Like any girl had a chance when he looked at them like that. She felt her cheeks heating up and looked over at the coffee table to set her plate down. *Focus.* She told herself. *Take a breath and ask a question. Yes, a question.* She took a sip of her wine.

"So, how long have you been working with Walter?" she asked.

"About seven years. He has always been my agent." Answered Sebastian.

Laura nodded. She couldn't seem to get her brain to function.

"Why do you work at Studio B?" asked Sebastian as he set his empty plate on the coffee table. They'd been throwing questions back and forth for a while now and knew each other's favorite colors, movies, books, music. He put a pillow behind his back and settled back against the armrest on the opposite side of the couch from Laura. He ran his hand over her left foot which was lying in his lap.

"That's easy. I like working at Studio B. I thought these were going to be hard questions." Answered Laura. She was amazed at how relaxed she felt around Sebastian. It was like they were old friends just catching up on each other's lives. She wasn't sure how her foot had ended up in his lap, but she couldn't complain about the massage that she was getting. Between that and the wine, she was very comfortable, indeed.

Sebastian shook his head. "That is not what I meant and you know it. You have been working with Matt for five years. That is a long time in this business."

Laura nodded. "Yes, it is. I'm happy where I am. I like working with Matt. He asks my opinions on things, and he really listens to what I have to say; I get a variety of work. I get a lot of freedom. I've worked on movies, done modeling, set up shows. I've done all kinds of things. I've learned a lot working with Matt."

"That is my point. You are obviously talented. Have you not ever thought of modeling or acting or having your own agency?"

"No. I don't want my own agency. I enjoy modeling sometimes, but it's not something that I want to do all the time. I've been in some movies, and I've turned down parts in movies. I have my own standards and I like it that way." She smiled at him. "Besides that, if I told Matt that I wanted to do acting or modeling, he'd give me jobs in a heartbeat. I'm just not interested in that right now."

"You are a very interesting person. Most people would want the money and recognition. Matt told me that you will not even let him show your pictures."

"I'm not interested in that type of recognition." Answered Laura.

"Is that why you are so cautious of being with me?" asked Sebastian, curiously.

"I just don't like my life public."

"Something happened to you." He guessed, studying her intently.

Laura glanced down at her hands, clenched in her lap. "Yes. Something happened to me."

"We don't have to talk about it." Said Sebastian, assuredly. He grabbed her other foot and placed it in his lap, then began massaging it. "I believe you have two questions for me."

Laura glanced up at him. "You really don't have any secrets, do you?"

Sebastian shook his head. "At this moment, you are the only secret I have."

"Why is that?" asked Laura.

"Because you don't want anyone knowing about us." Answered Sebastian, frowning.

"No. Why don't you have any secrets?"

"It is easier that way. There is nothing for anyone to dig up on you. Of course, you cannot convince people of that. They always think that you are hiding something." He shrugged. "I try not to do things that I would not want people to know about."

Laura studied him intently. She knew this had been a big mistake. She couldn't see Sebastian Thomas. He didn't even have secrets. She had a skeleton in her closet. This skeleton was the reason she didn't pursue modeling or acting. What would he think if he knew her secret?

--- ❧ ---

Laura flipped through the channels on the television and stopped when she saw Cary Grant on a cruise ship. "This is my favorite movie." She glanced at Sebastian. "*An Affair to Remember.*"

"I have seen it. It is a good movie. Want to watch it?" asked Sebastian, he slipped his arm around Laura's shoulders. "I am cold. Now you have to warm me up."

Laura laughed and spread the afghan over both of them. "Is that better?"

"Yes." He leaned over and nuzzled her hair. "You smell good. Like spring."

"Spring, huh?" asked Laura, glancing over at him. "You know that it's summer, right?"

Sebastian looked at her and smirked. "Not accepting compliments anymore?"

"Thank you." She said glancing down at the floor.

"You are very welcome." Said Sebastian. He glanced at the screen. "This part always amused me when they sat in the restaurant separately but seated next to each other."

Laura sighed. "I always thought this was such a romantic movie. They talk and get to know each other and fall in love."

Sebastian turned his head and looked into Laura's green eyes. "Yes. That is romantic. The walks on the deck in the moonlight. The day trip on the beach to meet his grandmother."

Laura smiled, pleased that he could talk about parts of the movie. "You have seen it."

Sebastian nodded. "Yes, it is also one of my favorite movies."

Laura studied his face for a moment longer and then turned back to the movie. *Breathe. Keep your feet on the ground.* She watched Deborah Kerr falling in love on screen.

--- ☙ ---

Sebastian sat on the couch, gazing down at Laura. They had stayed up late into the night watching television and talking. He was not sure when they had fallen asleep, but it had been before sunup. He glanced at his watch. The morning was almost over. His eyes traced over the curve of her cheek, her delicate nose, and her full lips that looked very soft. He could not resist smoothing her hair back off of her face, tucking an auburn strand behind her ear. What was it about this woman that had caught and kept his attention? Her phone rang and Sebastian glanced around but remembered seeing it on the kitchen bar. No way he could get to it without disturbing her.

Laura opened her eyes and looked up at him.

"Good Morning." Greeted Sebastian.

Laura sat up quickly and scooted away from him. "Good Morning." She glanced at the window. "I'm sorry I fell asleep on you."

Sebastian laughed. "I fell asleep, too."

Laura stood up. She wanted to keep distance between them, thinking that she probably didn't look so hot this morning and she didn't want to breathe on him before she had a chance to brush her teeth. "Um, I would like to get a shower and change. Would you like to go first?"

Sebastian smiled. "Why don't you go ahead? I have my luggage in the trunk of Matt's car. I can get it while you are in the shower."

Laura shook her head. "Not a good idea. I can get it for you." She was thinking of him being seen in the parking lot and then people, mainly television crews, but probably some fans showing up on her doorstep.

Sebastian nodded. "Sure. Okay. After your shower."

"Okay. I'll be quick." Answered Laura. She went into her room and closed the door. She couldn't believe that she had fallen asleep with Sebastian Thomas in her apartment. Was she crazy? She shook her head. *Get moving. He's waiting.* Laura grabbed some clothes and jumped into the shower. She was dressed and brushing her teeth when she realized that she didn't even know who had called this morning. She would check messages after she got Sebastian's things from the car. She checked herself in the mirror and then took a deep calming breath.

- - - ✿ - - -

She walked into the living room and glanced around. Something smelled good. She followed the smell to the kitchen.

Sebastian turned towards her when she walked into the kitchen. "I hope you don't mind. I thought I would cook us some brunch." He was cracking eggs into a bowl.

"It smells delicious." Replied Laura. "Of course, I don't mind. I certainly can't complain about you cooking me breakfast." She glanced at the clock and smiled. "Or lunch."

Sebastian poured some milk into the eggs and whisked them together, then poured them into the pan on the stove. "Everything will be ready in a few minutes."

"Anything I can do to help?" asked Laura.

"No, thank you. I snooped around the kitchen and found everything. You can just have a seat."

"I'll run out to the car and get your bag." Said Laura.

"Okay. I just need my duffel, please." Answered Sebastian as he stirred the eggs in the pan on the stove.

"Be right back." Laura watched him for a minute and then grabbed the car keys from the counter and went outside.

- - - ❡ - - -

Laura cleaned the kitchen while Sebastian took his shower and changed. She kept reminding herself that he was really there, and she wasn't dreaming. How odd it felt to know that he was in her apartment and he had cooked for her. But then it felt so natural for him to be there. She shook her head and smiled to herself. She didn't want to read too much into this. They had just had **one** date. How was she supposed to feel? Special, is how she felt. Yes. She'd just enjoy that feeling for now. Analyze things later when she was alone.

Her phone rang and she remembered that she hadn't checked messages, yet. She turned around to answer it and Sebastian walked into the room. She stopped and let her gaze travel over him for a moment. His hair was damp and messy, and he wore a pair of black jeans and a blue button-down shirt with the top two buttons undone. The phone rang, again and she grabbed it. "Excuse me." She said to him.

"Hello." Answered Laura.

"Hello, sleepy head. Did you just get up?" said Mandy. "You sound kind of breathless."

"No. I've been awake for a while. I was just cleaning the kitchen." Answered Laura.

"So, tell me how your casting call went yesterday."

"Can I call you back later?" asked Laura.

Mandy was quiet for a minute. "Do you have company?"

"Yes. I'll call you tonight."

"Oh, yeah you will. I want details." Said Mandy as she laughed and hung up.

Laura smiled and hung up the phone. She turned her attention to Sebastian who was standing in the doorway watching her. "Sorry about that. That was my best friend, Mandy. She would have kept calling all day until I answered."

"No problem. You could have talked to her." Answered Sebastian.

Laura shook her head. "I'll call her back later. She lives in Los Angeles, so Sundays are our catch-up days."

"What does she do?" asked Sebastian.

"She works for *LA Info*." Answered Laura. She waited for Sebastian's next question.

"Is she the one that wrote the story on the photographer scandal? Amanda Knight?"

Laura nodded. "That's her."

"She handled that story very well." Commented Sebastian.

"She only deals in facts. If she can't confirm it, then she won't write it. It has caused some tension between her and her boss, but Mandy refuses to write something that she can't verify."

"She has earned a lot of respect for that. Some of my friends have said that they will only talk to her."

"Mandy has definitely earned her place in the industry."

"Where did you meet her?" asked Sebastian.

"We grew up together. We graduated and then took our separate paths, but we keep in contact. We talk several times a week and then for hours on Sundays when we can."

"When is the last time that you have seen each other?"

"Last year. We met halfway for our birthday present to each other and spent the weekend together."

"Savannah, Georgia is a long way from Los Angeles, California."

"Yes. She's supposed to come and visit at the end of the month, but it depends on if she can get away. I was planning on sending her a plane ticket for her birthday." Laura explained.

"When is that?"

"May 15th. I just missed it. It's going to be a late present."

"Is your birthday the same day?" asked Sebastian.

Laura shook her head. "No. Mine is in June."

Laura spent the rest of the afternoon with Sebastian. They watched old movies on tv and chatted the whole afternoon, eating leftovers from their dinner the previous night. The day flew by and then Laura drove Sebastian to the car rental place to pick up his car. His agent, Walter, had set up a pick-up for Sebastian. The place was closed on Sunday, but they had a pick-up area and had arranged for Sebastian to get his car after hours. Of course, they didn't know the car was for Sebastian Thomas. The rental was under an alias. Totally legal and discreet.

- - - ℰℐ - - -

Laura glanced at the clock as the phone rang. She picked up the receiver and pulled her afghan around her. She held the afghan up to her nose and sniffed. It smelled like him. She giggled. She was acting like such a schoolgirl. "Hello."

"What is so amusing?" asked Mandy.

"Just laughing at myself." Answered Laura.

"Are you cracking up over there? I don't want to fly back to have you committed."

Laura laughed. "No. I'm fine. What's up?"

"Don't you dare what's up me? Who was at your place earlier?" demanded Mandy.

Laura smiled. Mandy always did get straight to the point. "You'll never guess."

"Did you have a date?" asked Mandy.

"Yes." Laura teased her friend, knowing she was waiting for details.

"With whom?"

"He just showed up at the agency." Explained Laura excitedly.

"Who did?" Mandy paused for a minute. "No. Are you talking about Sebastian Thomas?"

"Yes." Laura giggled as Mandy screamed into the phone.

"I want all the details." Demanded Mandy.

"Well, he showed up at the agency after the casting calls, delivering flowers. Then we went out to dinner. Then we went to my apartment and talked and watched *An Affair To Remember*." Laura knew she was talking fast and running everything together, but she was just so excited.

"Did he kiss you?"

Laura sighed. "Almost, but we got interrupted. Mandy, he is nice and funny and fun to be with. It just felt natural being with him. Like I'd known him for a while. It was just comfortable. We talked most of the night."

"Why was he at your place this morning? You didn't." exclaimed Mandy.

"No. We fell asleep on the couch watching a movie." Explained Laura.

"Wow. You had Sebastian Thomas in your apartment."

"I know. I almost can't believe it." Giggled Laura. "He also cooked for me."

"He cooked for you?" asked Mandy.

"Yes. He made me breakfast. It was very good."

"Nice, funny, sexy and can cook. Hmm. Sounds good to me." Said Mandy. "Are you going to see him, again?"

"He asked me out for Tuesday night." Answered Laura.

"So, what does that mean? Are you two officially dating?"

"He said that he wants to get to know me." Answered Laura. "His next movie is being filmed in Hilton Head."

"So, you two will get to see each other a little at least." Mandy laughed. "Wow. My best friend's dating Sebastian Thomas and I can't even write about it."

"No. You can't." replied Laura.

"Don't worry. I won't." said Mandy, then added. "Not until you tell me to."

Chapter Six

The next morning, Laura was up bright and early, ready to go to work. She stopped by the post office to get the mail and then picked up breakfast on her way to the office. She ate breakfast, sorted through the mail and opened up the office before Matt showed up. She hoped that was a good sign and that he was spending time with Elizabeth.

Laura glanced up as she heard the lobby door open. Matt and Elizabeth walked in laughing. Laura smiled and stood up. "How was your weekend?"

Elizabeth held up her left hand and smiled brightly. "Great!"

Laura admired the ring on her finger. "It's beautiful! Congratulations!"

Elizabeth laughed. "Matt proposed to me last night under the stars. We went out on his boat Saturday and stayed until this morning. It was very romantic and very private."

Laura smiled. "It sounds very romantic."

"I don't remember the last time that I have had such a relaxing weekend." Said Elizabeth. "It was perfect. He prepared a wonderful meal, and we picnicked on the deck under the stars."

She sighed. "He had the ring in a candy box with my favorite chocolates." She laughed. "Am I boring you?"

"No." insisted Laura. "I am so pleased that you would share it with me."

Elizabeth grabbed her hand. "Of course, Laura. You are one of my dearest friends." She smiled. "I haven't forgotten about your date. Did you have a good time?"

Laura giggled. "Yes. We had a great time." She glanced at Matt. "Did you know that he will be filming in Hilton Head?"

Matt nodded. "I had heard that."

Laura glanced at her desk. "Oh, here are your messages. I put your car keys on your desk and I filled up the tank. Thank you so much for letting us borrow your car."

"No problem." Answered Matt.

"Will you be seeing Sebastian, again?" asked Elizabeth.

Laura nodded, not being able to contain a smile. "Yes. He asked me out for tomorrow night."

- - - ↻ - - -

"So, what are you doing with your days?" asked Laura, as she and Sebastian sat at the boardwalk in downtown Savannah.

"Just exploring. No one knows that I am here, yet. I just wear a hat and sunglasses and try to blend in. It is a lot easier since this is a college town and there are so many eclectic people around. People don't pay that much attention to me."

"That would definitely make it easier. I didn't think of that." Laura glanced around at the people milling about. No one was paying them any attention. She glanced at Sebastian. "Let's go to the candy shop. They make saltwater taffy in the window. I love to watch it." Laura giggled. "And eat it."

Sebastian smiled. "Candy shop it is, then." They slipped into the throng of people walking up and down the boardwalk and stopped in front of the window of the candy shop. There was a machine in the window with taffy stretched across it, spinning and stretching the taffy.

"Do you like taffy?" asked Laura.

Sebastian glanced at her. "I don't know. I have never had any."

"What?" Laura laughed. "You have been deprived." She grabbed his arm. "Come on." She pulled him into the shop and then began filling a bag with various flavors of taffy. "Do you have a favorite flavor of anything? Like strawberry, orange, grape."

"Cinnamon." Answered Sebastian.

Laura glanced at him and nodded. "Okay." She tossed a few more pieces of taffy into the bag and then took it to the counter and paid for it.

"Would you like a sample, sir?" asked a lady standing next to the taffy machine.

"Sure." Answered Sebastian. He watched as the lady grabbed a stick and using the stick, pulled some taffy off of the machine and wound it around the stick. She did this twice and handed the two sticks to him. "Thank you." Said Sebastian. The lady smiled at him and glanced at Laura who had walked up beside him.

"Charming the ladies, are you?" Commented Laura.

Sebastian smiled and handed her one of the sticks. "There is only one lady that I am trying to charm."

Laura laughed. "I'll let you know if it works." They left the store and walked along the boardwalk, eating their taffy.

They walked past the souvenir shops, the tarot card reading booth, the jewelry shops and clothing stores, then stopped in front of the arcade and glanced at each other.

"Do you play air hockey?" Asked Laura.

Sebastian nodded. "Of course."

They spent the next couple of hours playing air hockey and competing in video games and pinball, then decided that it was time for dinner, so they walked down the boardwalk to a restaurant.

--- ❦ ---

"This has been such a wonderful evening." Said Laura. She glanced around the dimly lit restaurant, half expecting people to notice them and rush to the table to ask for autographs. "Thank you for inviting me."

"You are welcome. Thank you for coming. I have enjoyed tonight, also." Sebastian smiled at her. "Quit worrying about us being noticed."

"It's not that easy. It'll be in the papers that you are shooting a movie in Hilton Head. People will be looking for you."

"I know. I figured this would be our only time out on the town." Sebastian slipped some bills into the check folder and set it on the table. "Ready to get out of here?"

"Yes." Answered Laura.

They slipped out of their seats as the waiter walked up to their table. He nodded at them. "Thank you. Have a good evening." He picked up the folder and glanced inside, then glanced back at them.

"You, too." Answered Sebastian, smiling.

Laura laughed as they got outside. "What did you put in there?"

Sebastian smiled at her. "You saw his look of surprise, did you?"

"Yes."

"Let's just say that he got a nice tip."

"How generous of you, Mr. Thomas." Commented Laura as she felt their hands brush.

--- ❦ ---

"It's so beautiful out here at night." Commented Laura. They were standing on the boardwalk, looking out over the water. Most of the shops were closed for the night and lights were being turned off or dimmed, so they could see the stars clearly over the water.

"It is nice." Agreed Sebastian.

"So, how long is the filming scheduled for?" asked Laura.

"I think they said ninety-five days." Answered Sebastian. "They will not need me every day. I should be able to sneak away and visit."

"I'd like that." Answered Laura, glancing up at him. She glanced at her watch. "I didn't realize what time it is. Are you driving to Hilton Head tonight?"

"Yes. I will be fine." Sebastian smiled at her. "I am not ready to leave you, yet." He glanced at his watch. "Almost midnight. I guess we better get you back to your place, though."

Laura laughed. "Yes. Orange isn't my color."

- - - ❦ - - -

Sebastian pulled his car into a parking space beside Laura's parked car. What was he doing? He really should be going. She had to work the next day. He had a couple more days before they would start filming and he should be doing research. He sighed. Not really research. You couldn't research being an alien, but he wanted to prepare for the role. What would it feel like to be an alien on a planet that was not your own? You and your sister the only ones of your kind. Falling in love with a human and wanting to tell her, but not sure how? He turned his attention back to Laura. "I have a couple more days before everything gets hectic. Want to get together on Thursday?"

"Sure. Why don't you give me a call tomorrow and we'll figure out something to do?" answered Laura.

Sebastian nodded "Okay. I'll talk to you tomorrow, then." He started to get out of the car, but Laura stopped him.

"I'll be fine. You drive carefully. Talk to you later." She slipped out of the car, closed the door and hurried to her apartment.

Sebastian watched until she was inside and then backed out of his parking space and drove off.

Laura felt like she was literally on cloud nine as she got ready for bed and slipped into the covers. She fell asleep with his sexy smile playing through her mind.

- - - ↔ - - -

Laura's phone rang and she grabbed the receiver. "Hello."

"Hello, Laura." She heard Sebastian's deep voice come across the line.

"Hi, Sebastian. How was your day?" asked Laura.

"It was fine. I have been reading my script and preparing for my next role. How was your day?"

"Good. I've been looking forward to talking to you." She sighed. "Have you seen the paper, though?"

"No. Why?"

"There's talk of your movie and how you and several other actors will be in the area. So, no public outings for us."

"That is okay. I still want to see you, though. Any ideas?"

"I was going to suggest that we meet halfway, but that won't work now. People will be looking for you. Matt and Elizabeth invited us over for dinner, but I hate for you to drive all the way over here, again."

"It is not that far. We can have dinner with Matt and Elizabeth if you want. I can pick you up at your place and then we can drive over there together." Suggested Sebastian.

Laura sat quietly for a minute. "You know, it is only going to get harder for us to see each other."

Sebastian smiled. "Sometimes, yes. The only problem right now is where to meet. I think Matt's will be fine unless you don't want to go there."

"We can go to Matt's. I'd like to see you." Answered Laura. She had to admit to herself that she was having reservations about them having a relationship at all, but seeing Sebastian was winning the battle at the moment. It was much easier to resist temptation when he was across the United States and not within a hundred miles of her location.

"Great! What time shall I pick you up?" he asked.

Laura smiled to herself. Sebastian was always so fun to be with.

--- ❧ ---

Laura and Sebastian pulled up in front of Matt's house.

"He lives out here, huh?" asked Sebastian, glancing around at the woods, as they got out of the car and walked to the front door.

Laura glanced around. "Yeah. I love it out here. I like that he kept so many trees and didn't clear out all of the property."

"It is beautiful." Agreed Sebastian.

The door opened before they could knock, and Elizabeth smiled and hugged Laura. "Hi. Come in. I'm glad you could make it Sebastian."

"Thank you, Elizabeth. I hear congratulations are in order." Answered Sebastian.

"Thank you." Elizabeth started towards the kitchen. "Matt's back here."

Laura and Sebastian followed her into the kitchen where Matt was cooking. He turned around as they entered. "Hello. Glad you could make it."

Sebastian stepped forward and they shook hands. "Thank you for inviting me. Congratulations on your engagement." He handed a bottle of wine to Matt.

"Thank you." Matt admired the bottle. "Nice. Let's open this right now." He pulled some glasses from the cabinet and poured wine for everyone.

Matt held up his glass. "A toast. To friends."

"And new beginnings." Added Sebastian.

Everyone touched glasses and Laura's eyes caught Sebastian's. This man drove her crazy. How thoughtful of him to bring Matt and Elizabeth a gift and toast their engagement. He seemed to surprise her every time they saw each other.

--- ❧ ---

"That was one of the best meals I have ever eaten." Said Sebastian as he sat back in his chair.

"Yes. It was delicious, Matt." Agreed Laura.

"Thank you. I'm glad you enjoyed it." Said Matt.

Elizabeth smiled and stood up. "He is spoiling me." She started gathering plates from the table.

Matt smiled at Elizabeth. "You cook as much as I do."

Laura stood up and helped Elizabeth gather dishes, then followed her into the kitchen. "So, you two decided to keep Matt's place?"

"Yes. There's no way we would get rid of it. It's beautiful out here. Plus, Matt designed it himself. I couldn't even think to ask him to give it up."

Laura nodded in agreement as she glanced out the window at the trees outside. "It's very peaceful out here."

"I do enjoy coming home after work to the sounds of nature as opposed to the noise of the city." Agreed Elizabeth as she pulled dessert plates out of the cabinet. "Can you grab the pie out of the fridge?"

"Sure." Laura opened the fridge and found a chocolate pie on the bottom shelf. "Did you make this?"

Elizabeth nodded. "It's easy. Chocolate pudding and cool whip and graham cracker crust."

"Looks delicious." Laura followed Elizabeth to the dining room.

--- ∞ ---

"Are they doing open casting for extras or are they contacting the local agencies?" asked Matt, inquiring about the filming of Sebastian's new movie, *Worlds Apart*.

"I am not sure what Dan has decided to do." Answered Sebastian.

Laura glanced at Matt and then quickly away. It was only a matter of time before he came around her turf. She had hoped, never, but that didn't seem a possibility now.

"Dan? Dan Morris?" asked Matt.

"Yes. That's the director. He does not directly handle casting, of course, but he likes to put in his requests." Said Sebastian.

Matt nodded. "I've worked with him before."

Laura jumped up. "Wow! It's getting late. I'd better get you home." She turned to Elizabeth and Matt. "Thank you for dinner."

"Glad you could come." Said Elizabeth as she walked Laura and Sebastian to the door.

"See you at work tomorrow." Said Matt. He turned to Sebastian. "Good night."

"Good night." Answered Sebastian. "Thank you for inviting me."

Laura was quiet all the way back to her apartment. When Sebastian pulled into a parking space, she reached for the door handle, but Sebastian grabbed her arm.

"Are you okay?" asked Sebastian.

Laura smiled. "Yes. I had a great time. Thank you for going with me."

Sebastian studied her. "You can talk to me, you know."

"I'm fine. Just tired." Answered Laura. She put her hand over Sebastian's. "Really. I'm sorry."

"No. It is okay. I had a great time, too." He took his hand off her arm.

"Good. Be careful driving back to the hotel. I'll talk to you later?"

Sebastian nodded. "Yes. I'll call you."

"Good night." Laura slid out of the car and closed the door.

"Good night." Sebastian responded, puzzled at her mood change, as he watched her walk to her apartment door.

Chapter Seven

re you still going to be able to meet me in Brighton Beach tomorrow?" asked Sebastian.

Laura glanced at her watch and looked towards the set. It was almost midnight. "I think so. They're trying to get this last scene shot and then we'll be finished for the night. What time will you be there?"

"I will be there by ten. I will call you when I arrive." Answered Sebastian.

"Okay. Talk to you then."

"Laura, drive careful." Said Sebastian.

Laura smiled. "I'll be fine. You, too." She hung up her phone.

"Have you been to the set of *Worlds Apart*, yet?" Two of the female extras were walking by Laura.

"No. I heard that Sebastian's been giving autographs, though."

"Yeah. He does during breaks on the set, but afterwards, nobody ever sees him."

"Where do you think he goes?"

"He probably just stays in his hotel room. You know it's turned into grand central station in Hilton Head."

Laura smiled to herself and turned her attention back to the scene being filmed. Hopefully, **everyone** thought Sebastian was hiding in his hotel.

--- ‿ ---

Laura pulled her silver Chevy Malibu LTZ into the parking lot at Brighton Beach. She pulled into a parking space next to a black Toyota Camry. She glanced around and then watched as Sebastian stepped out of the Toyota, walked around her car and slid into the passenger seat. He glanced at the windows. "Nice."

She smiled. "I figured it would probably be a good idea to get the rest of the windows tinted. They put a light tint on the windshield, too. It helps with glare, but also keeps people from seeing clearly into the car." She turned towards him and eyed his baseball hat. "Nice hat." "

He gave her his one-sided grin. "I was hoping it would help."

She shrugged. "That depends on if they are specifically looking for you or not. So, what are we doing?"

"Not sure. Know anything about this area?" asked Sebastian.

Laura shook her head. "Not really." She glanced at the sky; the clouds looked ready to burst. "The beach will be empty soon, though. It's getting ready to rain."

No sooner than the words were out of her mouth, they heard the patter of raindrops as they hit the roof of the car and saw people gathering their things and running for their vehicles.

"How long do you think it will last?" asked Sebastian as he glanced out the window, watching people run to their cars.

"I don't know. The weatherman didn't say anything about a storm. "Want to wait and see?"

"Sure." He glanced at her. "How is the movie coming along?"

"Surprisingly well. Damon and Tara work well together. It's a couple of the other talent that we are having challenges with."

Sebastian nodded, knowingly. He knew some actors and actresses could be difficult to deal with. "How is Matt doing?"

Laura laughed. "He's driving me crazy, but I know he always stresses during the filming. I know how to handle him." She smiled. "I think Elizabeth does, too. He seems more mellow when he gets to the set in the mornings."

Sebastian laughed. "I bet she does." He glanced around. "The beach is pretty deserted, and it is only sprinkling, want to walk? I have a hooded jacket in the car that you could use."

"Sure, but you use that one. I've got one." Answered Laura. "I always keep one handy in case it rains."

They grabbed their jackets and walked to the beach. They made their way down to the water's edge and stopped to admire the view.

"How is your filming going?" asked Laura.

Sebastian reached over and grabbed her hand, and they started walking down the beach. "Good. It is an interesting story line. Aliens living on Earth with the humans, blending in. Some of the aliens do not even know what they are."

"Really, how's that possible?" asked Laura, curiously.

"They have a human parent and are raised by them."

"Which are you?" asked Laura.

"I am an alien-hybrid, raised by my alien parents, but my mother was impregnated by a human." Answered Sebastian. He glanced at her frown. "Read the book. I do not think I am explaining it correctly."

Laura nodded. "I'll have to pick that one up." She glanced up, letting her hood slide off her head. "It's stopped raining." She bent down into the water and splashed some at Sebastian, giggling.

He grinned at her with a wicked gleam in his eyes. "You want to play, do you?" He stepped towards her.

Laura's eyes widened. "I was just kidding." She backed up but realized that she was just getting deeper into the water. She tried to dart past Sebastian, but he caught her around the waist and pulled her to him, laughing. "You won't melt, will you?" He swung her up into his arms and walked deeper into the water.

Laura tightened her arms around his neck. "Sebastian, you wouldn't, would you?" she glanced down at the water and then up into his face. Their gazes caught and the mischievous glint disappeared and something else replaced it. There was an intensity in his blue eyes and Laura couldn't tear her gaze away from his. She smelled cinnamon on his breath and felt its warmth on her face. She vaguely felt the rain start up again as Sebastian bent towards her and touched his lips gently to hers. She sighed as she felt the softness of his lips and felt the heat spread though her body as it reacted to his nearness. Her fingers curled into the hair at the back of his neck and she gave into the kiss, her body sagging into his. So many times, they'd come close, but never quite made it. It was so much better than she could have dreamed. She felt the hard muscles of his chest and arms as he held her there above the water. He pulled back and looked into her eyes and she tightened her hold on his neck, pulling his mouth back down to hers. Mmm. He tasted of cinnamon, too.

"Hey!" Someone yelled and they jerked apart. "There's a wave coming!"

Laura and Sebastian glanced towards the water and flinched as the wave moved towards them. The tide was coming in, so the waves were getting closer to the shore. There was no way for them to get out of the water before the wave hit, so Sebastian spun around and planted his feet into the sand and bent over Laura to keep her from getting the full force of the wave. The wave hit them, and Laura felt Sebastian's footing slip, but he kept them up. Luckily, it hadn't been too tall, but they were both soaked as the water hit Sebastian in the back and then broke over them. Laura looked up into Sebastian's face. His eyes held hers and he bent down and kissed her, again. Laura tightened her hold on Sebastian and let herself get lost in the kiss. Moments later, they pulled apart breathless, staring into each other's eyes. After a moment, Sebastian headed back towards the shore, Laura still in his arms.

"Thank you." Said Laura as Sebastian reached the shore. He walked a little ways down the beach and then set her down, then turned and waved thanks to the person who had yelled at them. He grabbed her hand and they started back to their cars.

- - - ℰℬ - - -

There was a knock on her door and the phone rang at the same time.

Laura grabbed the phone and went to answer the door. "Hello."

"Happy Birthday!" Exclaimed Mandy. "What is that hunk of a boyfriend doing for your birthday?"

Laura laughed at her friend. "Hold on, Mandy. Someone's at the door."

Laura glanced through the peep hole and then opened the door. "What are you doing here?" She stepped back from the door, glancing over his attire. She didn't think the hat and sunglasses would suffice if anyone studied him too closely.

Sebastian smiled as he followed her inside, then pulled her close for a kiss. "Surprise."

Laura smiled. "Hold that thought. Mandy's on the phone."

Sebastian nodded and went back to the door. He grabbed some bags that he had left outside and brought them in and set them on the counter.

Laura watched him curiously. "Thank you, Mandy." Answered Laura as she got back on the phone. The phone was silent and then a dial tone came on. Laura frowned and turned to Sebastian. "That's odd. She hung up."

"Oh, I forgot one thing." Sebastian went back out the door and stepped outside, then stepped into the doorway.

"Close your eyes." He prompted.

Laura sighed. "Sebastian, really."

"Close your eyes." He repeated.

Laura sighed, again, but closed her eyes. She knew Sebastian wasn't going to let her see his surprise until she did. She heard the door close and then someone stepped in front of her.

"Now, you can open them." Sebastian whispered, his mouth close to her ear, but she felt him behind her, so who was in front of her? She opened her eyes to see Mandy.

"Surprise!" Mandy hugged her and giggled. "I couldn't miss your birthday."

Laura laughed. "I'm so glad to see you, but I thought you couldn't come."

Mandy smiled at Sebastian. "Sebastian sent me a ticket."

Laura turned to Sebastian. "Thank you."

Sebastian's eyes twinkled. "You should be with your best friend for your birthday." He glanced at the clock. "Sorry I could not throw you a big party, but Matt and Elizabeth will be here shortly, so we need to get everything ready."

Laura looked at Sebastian and Mandy, happy to be with the two of them. "What can I do?"

Sebastian took her hand and led her to the couch. "You can sit and relax. Mandy and I have everything under control."

Laura sighed and sat on the couch as she was told. She pulled Sebastian to her and kissed him gently on the lips. "Thank you."

He trailed a finger down her cheek tenderly. "You are very welcome."

- - - ☙ - - -

Laura watched Mandy and Sebastian cooking in the kitchen and setting out trays of food on the table. An hour later when Matt and Elizabeth arrived, everything was ready. Matt set a cake on the counter and Elizabeth took it out of the box, so everyone could see it. It was a standard quarter sheet cake done in purple and white decorated with lilies.

"Looks delicious." Commented Laura.

Matt smiled at Elizabeth. "She wouldn't let me try it, so I don't know.'"

Laura turned to Elizabeth in surprise. "You made it? It's beautiful. Thank you."

Elizabeth hugged her. "Making cakes is my hobby. Happy Birthday."

--- ❦ ---

Laura watched her friends talking and laughing, sitting in the living room. She watched as Matt slipped his arm around Elizabeth and kissed her. They were a great couple. Matt with his olive skin tone and dark hair matched well with Elizabeth's petite blonde form. They'd been together for several years. Laura smiled as the light caught the diamond on Elizabeth's finger and made it sparkle. The two were great for each other. She was glad that Matt hadn't waited. Elizabeth was so happy she was glowing.

It was so nice to see her friends together and happy. She was thrilled that Mandy had made it. She hadn't seen her friend in over a year. Talking on the phone was nice but seeing each other in person was so much better. She glanced at Sebastian, who was talking to Matt and Elizabeth. Her gaze trailing over his jean clad muscular legs and up to his blue button-down shirt. She was very fond of the shirts he wore. They fit very nicely. She smiled as he glanced at her and winked.

--- ❦ ---

"So, tell me how things are going." Prompted Mandy.

Laura and Mandy were curled up on the couch. Matt and Elizabeth had left hours earlier and Sebastian had just left, having an early start scheduled for the next morning. Laura smiled at her friend and wrapped an afghan around herself. "Everything is fine so far."

Mandy frowned at her friend. "What does that mean?"

"It means that we are taking things one day at a time. We'll see how things go." Explained Laura. Leave it to Mandy, the journalist, to dig for details.

"Are you two serious?" asked Mandy, studying her friend.

"We've only known each other a couple of months. No, we're not serious. We're getting to know each other."

"You two look good together. You both seem happy, too." Said Mandy sincerely.

"Thank you for that." Said Laura. "I am happy. I didn't think that I'd be interested in dating anyone, but I like spending time with Sebastian. He is fun to be with and he is very down to earth. We can just sit and chat for hours or watch a movie and it's comfortable. I don't feel like I have to come up with something to talk about all of the time. You know what I mean? With some people, it's just uncomfortable to be together and not talk. With us, it's just not like that. I think we appreciate the time that we get to spend together."

Mandy nodded in understanding. "Yeah. I do know what you mean. I hope I meet someone like that someday."

"I know you will." Said Laura.

"Yeah. I will." agreed Mandy.

--- ☙ ---

Laura unlocked the door to *Studio B* and stepped inside. She walked down the hall to the storage room and flipped on the light. Matt needed some equipment. Laura glanced at her list. Hand-operated camera, dolly, video lights, extra extension cord and some miscellaneous props.

"Do you need any help?"

Laura jumped and knocked over a box as she spun towards the voice.

Sebastian grabbed the box before it could hit the floor.

"Sebastian!" exclaimed Laura. "You scared me half to death."

Sebastian looked sheepish "Sorry. I thought you heard me come in."

"Laura!"

Laura and Sebastian turned at the voice.

"Quick." Laura motioned to the door across the hall. "Go in Matt's office."

Sebastian slipped into the office just as Justin walked around the corner. "Matt sent me to help you get everything."

"Oh. Well, I think the camera is in the photography studio. Why don't you get that while I finish going through the closet?" suggested Laura.

"Sure." Answered Justin. He walked around the corner to the photography studio and Laura stepped into Matt's office.

"What are you doing here?" asked Laura.

"I was coming to see you when I saw your car pull in here, so I thought I would just surprise you." Said Sebastian.

"You definitely surprised me." Answered Laura. "Won't you be missed?"

Sebastian shook his head. "They don't need me today. They rearranged some scenes to accommodate Danny Long."

"Oh. He's in the movie, too? Cool."

Sebastian raised an eyebrow, inquisitively. "Are you a fan of his, as well? Should I be jealous?"

Laura smiled, placed her hand on his chest and pushed Sebastian gently against the wall, then stood on her tiptoes and placed her lips on his. The kiss quickly deepened, and Laura slid her arms around his neck.

Sebastian placed his hands on her waist and pulled her against him. Laura felt like she was going to explode. Everywhere his body touched hers, her body pulsed with need.

They pulled apart, breathless. Laura stepped back and smiled sexily. "Do you think that you need to be jealous?"

Sebastian leaned against the wall and ran his hand through his hair. "Woman, you drive me crazy."

Laura laughed and pulled her keys out of her pocket. "Think you can sneak into my place? I can meet you there later."

Sebastian took her keys. "I will be waiting."

Laura watched the scene play through and smiled to herself. Damon added a tough guy attitude to the scene that hadn't been in the script, but it seemed to work well. He seemed to really enjoy his role.

Laura watched Lance and Matt discuss the scene after it was finished and Lance was smiling.

"I definitely came to the right place." Said Lance. He glanced at Laura. "I'm still having fun."

Laura laughed. "I'm glad to hear it." She turned to Matt. "Think I could sneak away for a couple hours?"

Lance smiled mischievously. "Got a hot date?"

Matt glanced up from the papers he was reading. "Everything okay?"

Laura nodded. "Yeah. He just got an unexpected break." She glanced around. "I was hoping to sneak away for a long dinner. I'll be back."

Matt smiled. "I think we can survive without you for the evening."

"Are you sure?" asked Laura. "I don't want to leave you hanging."

Matt glanced down at his papers. "There's only one more scene scheduled for tonight. We'll be fine."

"Great! Thanks. I'll see you in the morning." Answered Laura as she spun around and headed for her car.

--- ✑ ---

Laura let herself into her apartment and stopped inside the doorway. Something smelled good. Sebastian was going to spoil her if he kept cooking for her. She headed for the kitchen and laughed as she saw all the packages strewn over the counter.

"I thought you were cooking." Said Laura.

Sebastian smiled sheepishly at her as she walked over to him. "I cheated. You are just in time, though. The food just arrived." He kissed her. "Mama said to tell you hello and not to be a stranger."

"Yeah. I've been too busy to go to the restaurant the last few weeks. Either that or it's too late when we finally finish for the night." She glanced around at his preparations for dinner. "Do you mind if I take a quick shower?"

"No. Go ahead. I'll just set the table and unpack things." Sebastian turned the oven dial to warm.

"I'll be quick." Laura dashed out of the kitchen and to her room, stripping as soon as she closed the door.

Sebastian set the table and poured some wine, then put the salads on plates and placed them on the table. He was on his way back to the kitchen when Laura came down the hall. All he could do was stop and stare at her as she approached and smiled at him. She was wearing form fitting jeans and a green button-down shirt. He swallowed and watched her walk into the room. He was glad to have her in his life. She seemed like the only sane and uncomplicated thing in his life at the moment. "Ready to eat?"

"Yes." Said Laura. "What can I do?"

"Just have a seat." Said Sebastian as he pulled out her chair. She sat down and he pushed her chair in. "I'll grab the breadsticks and be right back."

- - - ♋ - - -

Laura took a sip of her wine. "You are going to spoil me."

"You deserve to be spoiled." Replied Sebastian.

Laura glanced across the table at him. She felt like a silly schoolgirl. She just wanted to smile. It was still hard to fathom sometimes that he was in her apartment, having dinner with her. That she was dating Sebastian Thomas. They acted like normal couples. Having dinner, watching movies, talking on the phone. When would it end, though? This wouldn't last forever. Maybe, it was just a temporary thing for him. A little fling with the local woman while filming a movie in her town. Maybe it just gave him something to do other than hide out in his hotel room. She frowned. He had a much more glamorous life than that. He didn't really need her.

"What are you thinking about?" asked Sebastian.

Laura sighed. "Do you really want to be here?" she glanced at her plate. "I mean, what happens to us when you leave? This is just a fling, isn't it?"

Sebastian looked at her across the table. "Which question would you like me to answer first?"

Laura glanced up at him. "Take your pick."

Sebastian set down his fork. "Okay. Yes. I really want to be here. I certainly would not be otherwise. I was invited to hang out with some friends tonight but chose to be here with you instead." He reached across the table and took her hand. "As far as what happens to us when I leave, I am not entirely sure. I do want to see you. I am not anxious to leave you, but I do have other obligations. Interviews and such have already been scheduled for promoting our movie." He reached his other hand across the table and took hers. "No. This is not just a fling. I really care about you. I enjoy spending time with you, and I hope that you feel the same."

Laura stared at him for a moment and then glanced down at their hands, their fingers interlocked. "I'm sorry. I didn't mean to put you on the spot. I wasn't trying to get a declaration of love from you."

Sebastian smiled at her. "You didn't put me on the spot. I know what you meant. Everything is fine."

"You're too good for me, Sebastian." Said Laura.

Sebastian shook his head. "I don't believe that for a second."

--- ⁊ ---

Sebastian glanced around at the crowds of people around the area and sighed. There seemed to be more and more each day. It was kind of overwhelming. He hoped that he brought enough to the character for it to be what the fans wanted. If he didn't, well, they certainly wouldn't want him in the second film. He smiled and walked over to the line that cordoned off the area. Magazines and notebooks were thrust at him. He pulled his pen out of his pocket and began signing autographs and shaking hands.

"So, Sebastian, where do you keep sneaking off to?" asked Michael as he and Laura Fraser walked up to him after they finished signing autographs and talking to the fans.

"Just getting some peace and quiet and running lines. Working on the character." Answered Sebastian.

Laura and Michael glanced at each other. "So, if we come by later, you'll be in your room?" asked Michael.

Sebastian smiled. "Not tonight. I have plans."

"Want some company?" asked Laura.

Sebastian glanced at his friends. "Not tonight. No. Thank you, though."

"If you're not careful, man, people are going to think that you are antisocial." Said Michael.

"We will get together later." Responded Sebastian as he walked away toward the set.

--- ∞ ---

Laura glanced up as someone knocked on her car window. She smiled and closed the book that she had been reading as Sebastian slid into the passenger seat of her car.

Sebastian leaned over and kissed her. "Hi. How are you doing?" he picked up the book. "What do you think?"

Laura glanced at the cover of *Worlds Apart*. "It's very interesting. If I didn't have plans with you, I'd probably be at home reading it."

Sebastian nodded. "I thought it was interesting, too. She is actually still working on the books. I think there is supposed to be eight or ten in the series."

"I can see that. I'm only on chapter two, but I already like the characters. I would definitely want to read more about them."

"I am sure the author would be happy to hear that."

Laura smiled at Sebastian. "Enough promoting. What are we doing tonight?"

"Not sure." Sebastian shrugged. "We are running out of places to sneak off to."

Laura laughed. "We're going to have to be more creative." She glanced around the beach. They had decided to meet at Brighton Beach, again. The sun was setting, and the sky was streaked with shades of pink and purple. She felt Sebastian's hand slide into hers and he gently squeezed her fingers.

Laura's gaze remained fixed on the sky. "It's beautiful, isn't it?"

"Yes. You are." Sebastian whispered into her ear.

Laura turned her head and found her face mere inches from his. His cinnamon breath warm on her cheek. "You trying to hit on me, Mr. Thomas?" she whispered back, trying to lighten the mood. He was slipping right into her heart, and she wasn't ready for it.

Sebastian smiled. "Depends. Is it working?"

Laura angled her body towards his and leaned across the console. "I think it might be." She pressed her lips to his and thought about how she could stay like this forever. Here with Sebastian, shut off from the world.

--- ❦ ---

After several months of text messaging, e-mailing, and secret dates, Laura knew that she was falling in love with Sebastian. He'd managed to sneak away a few times to see her since they were filming in Hilton Head, which was only about an hour away from Savannah. She'd also managed to meet him a couple of times but outside of Hilton Head. Of course, they'd both been working twelve-to-fourteen-hour days, so they were exhausted, but they enjoyed each other's company. She'd stayed busy with the filming of

Dawn's Cover and was relieved that this was the last week of filming. She grabbed a sandwich from the snack table and sat under a tree, watching one of the scenes being shot from there. She wasn't close enough to hear, but she had a clear view from where she sat.

She thought about what Matt had told her earlier. He was getting more insistent on her doing modeling jobs and she felt that Sebastian was partially to blame for that. Sebastian and she had had dinner with Matt and Elizabeth a few times while he was visiting, and Sebastian had asked Matt why he never had Laura do any jobs. Of course, this brought up a conversation on what she had actually done, and Matt decided that she should move to bigger things. Laura sighed as they wrapped up the scene and she watched the crew start packing things up for the day. She got up and made her way over to Matt.

"You're still here?" asked Matt. "I thought you had left already. Weren't you supposed to have a date tonight?"

Laura shook her head. "I cancelled. It's our last week. I need to be here."

Matt smiled at her. "Go home. We're starting at seven in the morning."

"The gear-"

Matt interrupted her. "Will be taken care of. Go home."

Laura held up her hands. She knew when not to argue with the boss. "Okay. Good night." Laura grabbed her bag and made her way to her car. She drove straight home and went straight to the shower as soon as she got home, then crawled into bed.

Her phone played a jingle, and she knew that Sebastian had messaged her. She got up, dug her phone out of her bag and climbed back into bed. She opened the message. *Hello Beautiful. Are you on-line?*

Laura shook her head. She'd been thinking about how things were going with her and Sebastian lately and knew that they needed to stop. Did she care about him? Yes. That's exactly why she needed to tell him that they couldn't see each other anymore. He had no secrets. She had one. A big one. She didn't want to ruin his reputation with her horrible secret.

One reputation was enough to ruin. There were only two other people who knew- Matt and Mandy. No one else. Mandy knew because she was Laura's best friend and had helped her get through the toughest time in her life. Matt knew because he had kind of saved her at a time in her life when she had nothing left. Now, she just had to figure out how to tell Sebastian that they were through.

Her phone jingled again. *Are you there?*

Laura smiled. He was persistent. And boy, did she love him. *Yes. I'm logging on now.* Laura climbed out of bed and sat down in front of her desk where she had left her laptop the night before. She sighed and logged into her IM.

S: I thought maybe you were sleeping.

L: I just got home.

S: You were shooting that late tonight?

L: Yes. We'll restart at 7. What about you?

S: I have tomorrow off. Then we only have three more days.

L: I think we've got tomorrow and half of the next day.

S: I was hoping to see you tomorrow.

L: I can't get away tomorrow. Sorry.

S: I understand.

L: How's everything else?

S: Good. I am going to have to leave, though on Saturday. We have an interview in New York for *Worlds Apart*.

L: That's great. Sounds like the movie is going to be interesting.

S: Yes. It is interesting. I think it will turn out well. You are missing my point, though. If I do not see you tomorrow, I will not be able to see you for a couple of weeks.

L: I understand. That's how things are.

S: The premiere for *Truth or Dare* will be in two weeks. Will you go with me to that?

Laura sighed and closed her eyes. Don't promise anything. She opened her eyes and stared at the words, then typed a reply.

L: I don't think that's a good idea.

S: We have been seeing each other for a while now. I would like for you to be on my arm in public. I would like everyone to know who Laura is.

L: I don't think that's a good idea, either.

S: What does that mean?

L: I just think that maybe we should move on. You've got your life and I've got mine. It's not working.

S: What are you talking about? I just saw you two days ago, and everything was fine. What has happened?

L: I just don't want to drag you down with me. Look, I've got to go. 7 is going to come early. Good night.

Laura signed off and climbed into bed, wiping tears off of her cheeks. She was not going to cry. It didn't matter if her heart was breaking. Sebastian was better off without her.

- - - ℰ℈ - - -

Sebastian stared at the words on the screen. *I just don't want to drag you down with me.* This was about that damn secret that she had. Well, he did not care what it was. He had tried to find out. He had googled Laura Steele. She had been a model six years ago. Then she had disappeared. No reason why. There had been speculation, but nothing solid. What would make someone quit their career? She had been called the next hottest fashion model. She had companies lined up to sign her and she had just walked away from all of it. Now, she was an agent assistant. There were a couple articles about how her talent was wasted sitting behind a desk. People had tried to interview her, but she had declined. Sebastian logged off and picked up the phone and dialed. If Laura did not want to see him, fine, but she was going to tell him that to his face.

He listened to the phone ring on the other end. "Hello."

"Hi, Elizabeth. It's Sebastian. I am sorry to call so late. I just spoke to Laura, and she said that they had just finished filming. Could I speak to Matt?" Sebastian spoke calmly into the phone. More calmly than he felt. He had known that he cared for Laura, but now he realized just how much.

"Sure. He just walked in. Hold on, Sebastian."

Sebastian heard Elizabeth say something to Matt and then he came onto the phone.

"Hi, Sebastian. Is everything okay?" asked Matt, sounding concerned.

"I am not sure. How does Laura seem to you?"

Matt was quiet for a minute. "Fine. Why?"

"She is acting strange. Something about not wanting to drag me down with her. What does that mean? I know that you know."

"I think you should ask Laura that question." Matt sighed. "I'm sorry, Sebastian. I can't explain that to you. Laura will have to. It's a private matter."

"There is filming tomorrow?"

"Yes. Tomorrow should be our last full day." Answered Matt, cautiously.

"I will be there tomorrow, Matt. I will talk to her in front of everyone if I have to."

"That wouldn't be a good idea. Why don't you come to my house, and I'll send her here to get something? You can't have this conversation in public. It would ruin her."

"Just tell me this. Is this the reason that she doesn't model or act?"

"Yes. I warned you not to hurt her. Don't do this if you can't handle it. I do not want to have to pick up the pieces, again. She almost didn't make it back together last time."

"I am in love with her, Matt."

"I hope you mean that." Said Matt. "I'll see you tomorrow. I'll ask Elizabeth to wait for you before she leaves the house."

"Thank you, Matt."

"Just remember what I said. If you don't show up tomorrow, I understand. Good night."

Chapter Eight

$\mathcal{L}$aura tried to concentrate on the set all morning, but Sebastian kept slipping into her mind. The long nights, sitting on her couch, quizzing each other about their lives. The first time they had kissed on the beach. She shook her head. Snap out of it.

- - - ❧ - - -

"Laura. Just the person that I was looking for." Luke stopped in front of her. "I was looking for some of the equipment from last night and it's not where it usually is. I need an extension cord."

Laura stood up from her seat next to the tree. She needed to get her head into work. Not her troubles. "Unfortunately, I didn't clean up last night. I'll help you look for it." Laura led the way to one of the equipment trailers.

"Are you okay?" asked Luke.

Laura smiled. "Sure. Why?" She started looking in a plastic crate against the wall.

Luke shook his head. "You just seem distracted." He cleared his throat. "I've been meaning to ask you. Filming is almost over and-"

"Here it is. An extension cord for the lights. That's what you needed right?" Laura held a cord out to him.

Luke nodded. "Yes. Thank you." He accepted the cord and stood in front of the doorway. "I was wondering if you'd be interested in going out tomorrow night?"

Laura looked at Luke, surprised. Where had that come from? She blinked and smiled at him. "Thank you, Luke, but no. I'm seeing someone." At least she was until last night.

Luke smiled. "That's not surprising. Well, I'd better get to the set with this cord." He stepped out of the trailer.

Laura followed him out and watched him walk away.

Maybe she should get out of the entertainment industry all together. She would never feel comfortable with anyone that was in it. She would always worry about her secret interfering with other people's lives, too. She turned and caught Matt looking at her. He waved her over. Elizabeth walked up to him just as Laura reached him.

"Hi, Elizabeth. I see he dragged you out here this morning." Said Laura, forcing a smile.

Elizabeth shook her head. "I was coming this way to meet him for lunch."

Matt kissed Elizabeth. "Did you bring the box?"

Elizabeth frowned. "I'm sorry, honey. I forgot it by the door. I knew I forgot something."

Matt smiled at her. "That's okay. Laura, would you mind running out to my place and getting it?"

"Not at all, Matt. Is that all you needed?" Laura asked, wondering why Matt had called her over before speaking to Elizabeth.

"Yes, I think so." Said Matt, glancing at Elizabeth. Laura frowned. "Okay. I'll be back in a half hour."

"Take your time. Get some lunch if you want." Suggested Matt. He held out his house keys to her. "Here you go."

Laura took the keys and left. Matt was acting strangely. She gave herself a mental shake. It was probably just her, reading something in nothing. She got into her car and drove to Matt's. She parked in front of his garage and got out of her car, glancing around. She always loved it out here. It was so quiet and peaceful. No neighbors. Matt had a house built on ten acres and had kept the woods surrounding three sides of the house. He had built the house back from the road, so it had a secluded feel, even though it was ten minutes from town.

Laura unlocked the door and stepped inside, then glanced around the entry way, but didn't see a box. Didn't Elizabeth say that it was by the door? She shrugged and went into the kitchen. Usually, things ended up on the kitchen table or in Matt's office. She didn't find anything on the table, either. She walked down the hall to Matt's office and checked there, but didn't find a box, so she decided to do a quick check of the house. If Matt said he needed the box, then he needed it, and she didn't want to go back without it. She stepped into the living room and stopped in the doorway.

- - - ∽ - - -

"Hello, Laura." Said Sebastian. He was standing by the couch, looking way better than she wanted him to, wearing jeans and her favorite red button-down shirt. His hair was disheveled, like he'd been running his hands through it. Just like he was doing at that very moment.

"What are you doing here?" asked Laura, fearing she already knew. She'd been duped. There was no box.

"I wanted to talk to you." Answered Sebastian as he walked over to her.

"About what?"

"What you said last night. Something about dragging me down with you."

Laura shook her head in denial. "I don't remember saying that. I just said that we shouldn't see each other anymore."

"Right. After I asked you to go to a movie premiere with me. Will you not tell me what you are so afraid of?"

Laura avoided his eyes and looked down at the floor. "I'm not afraid of anything. We said we'd see how things were going and things aren't going well."

"The only problem I have is not seeing you enough." Responded Sebastian softly.

"I just don't want to see you anymore." Laura kept her face averted and squeezed her eyes shut. *Don't cry. Don't cry. Don't cry.* She repeated silently in her head.

Sebastian placed one hand on each side of her face, cupping her head between his palms and tilted her face towards him. "Look me in the eye and say it."

Laura kept her eyes closed as tears seeped from under her lids. "Don't make me."

Sebastian kissed each of her eyelids. "Baby, why are you crying?"

Laura opened her eyes and looked into his concerned gaze. "You were just supposed to take my word and go away. You weren't supposed to come here."

"If that is what you really want. I will. I will go away. You just have to say the words. Say them to me, not on the computer." Said Sebastian.

Laura could see the hurt in his eyes. She tried to form the words, but they wouldn't come out.

"I can't." She whispered.

"Ah, baby." Sebastian pulled her into his arms. "Tell me what is wrong, please. I can't stand to see you cry."

Laura buried her face in his shoulder and took a breath, calming herself. He wouldn't just walk away. He might after she told him. That would be for the best, though. Wouldn't it? Laura pulled away and nodded. "Okay. I'll tell you and then you'll be ready to walk away."

"Do you think that little of me?" asked Sebastian, frowning.

"No. I think that much of you. That's why I've tried to keep you out of this." She walked over to the couch and sat down. She waited for Sebastian to get settled beside her and then she started talking.

"You always ask me why I don't model or act as a career. Well, I used to model full time. Six years ago, I had a contract with a major company and traveled to Paris and Milan. I was in numerous magazines and did photo shoots in different locations all over the world. My agent turned down jobs for me because I was so busy. I was offered an acting part after I had some small parts in a couple of movies. I auditioned just like everyone else and was cast in a role.

The director, his assistant and the casting director offered me the lead. I hadn't auditioned for the lead, but another part. One of my friends had been given the lead and I knew this, so I refused. The directors didn't like this, but what could they do? Fire my friend? Then they'd have to fire me, too, because I still wouldn't take the job.

Well, the part that I was cast in was a bad girl role. I was the other woman and got caught with my friend's husband. She was supposed to catch us in bed. They wanted me to go nude for this scene. I tried negotiating this and they said they would agree to partial covering. I would wear underwear under the covers and only my breasts would be out of the covers, but I could wear a lacy bra. So, the parts that I was concerned about would be covered."

Laura glanced up to see Sebastian's expression. He just smiled in encouragement and nodded for her to continue.

"The morning the scene was to be filmed, I went in a little early to go over my lines and get changed into wardrobe. That was a mini skirt and halter top. Nothing flashy. I practiced my lines in the room set up for the scene and Dan showed up. He was one of the directors. He said he'd go over my lines with me. I declined, but he insisted, so I agreed just to keep the peace. He was the only one of the three directors who had stuck to the idea of the scene needing to be nude. We'd been over the scene a couple times, and I was comfortable with it, so he wanted to do the bedroom scene. I immediately turned him down. I was already uncomfortable being in my underwear on camera and I didn't feel the need to do this when the cameras weren't rolling.

Dan got offended and said that I wasn't the director. That I thought that I was so special that I could just come in and change the movie to my specifications. I told him that wasn't so. If he wanted the scene nude, he could have it, but not with me. Then I walked away from him." Laura took a deep breath as the images flashed through her head of that day.

Sebastian pulled her close and wrapped his arms around her. "You don't have to say anymore. It's okay."

Laura pulled away. "This is the part you'll want to hear."

Sebastian shook his head. "I don't think so."

"This is my reason for quitting." Laura looked into his deep blue eyes a moment longer and then tore her gaze away from his and focused on a picture of a meadow on the wall. In her mind, she saw that day at the studio.

"Dan didn't like that I had walked away from him. He didn't like the fact that I had changed the contents of the scene. Two of the directors had sided with me. He was the lead director of the movie. He felt his word was gospel. You see, he didn't let me walk away from him. He grabbed me and threw me onto that bed. Then he had his scene. He ripped every piece of clothing that I was wearing to shreds. I fought him. I punched and I scratched, and I screamed, but no one was there. No one heard me. For every punch or scratch that I got on him, he hit me. Then when he was finished, he left me there, bleeding on the bed. He walked away and left like nothing had even happened. I tried to get up, but I could barely move. Two of my ribs were broken and my wrist was fractured. I managed to pull the covers over me, but I couldn't get out of the bed. Tyler Daniels was playing the male lead and he found me. He helped me get some clothes on and took me to the hospital, and then he called my agent. I was also dating Tyler at the time, but it didn't last. He didn't understand how I could be raped, and he didn't want this tied to his career. He was moving up and he thought the story would harm his options."

"Oh my god, Laura. I am so sorry." Sebastian reached for her, but Laura jumped up and started pacing the living room.

"I don't blame him. They recast my role in the movie and Dan got the scene he wanted. I found out later, he had a video of that day. He didn't show it to anyone, but he said he kept it for his viewing pleasure. He said if I told anyone, he would make sure that it was seen by everyone. It was my word against his. Matt wanted me to press charges, but I knew the media would have a field day with this. Dan had doctored the video and I wasn't sure that I would be believed if anyone saw it. He sent me a clip of it one day and it didn't look like I was resisting. I'm sure that was after I had a fractured wrist and broken ribs, but no one would stop to ask questions. So, I quit modeling and stopped acting and took Matt's assistant job. I couldn't work with that over my head. At any time, Dan could decide to show that video. I couldn't do that to Matt."

Sebastian walked over to her and pulled her into his arms. "You are so worried about everyone else. What about you?"

"I'm fine. I got through it." She let herself relax in his warm embrace for a few moments and then pulled away and looked up into his face. "You see now, don't you? I can't let this get out. If I were to model or act, then Dan could decide to show the video. It would ruin me and everything that I worked for. It would hurt your career if you were associated with me. I can't do that to you." Laura turned away, not wanting to look at him when he told her that she was right. They shouldn't be together. It would hurt his career.

"Laura, look at me." Sebastian gripped her shoulders gently. "I am not going anywhere. You are not at fault for this. Matt was right. You should have pressed charges. Matt was your agent?"

Laura nodded. "Yes."

"Where is this Dan guy now?" Sebastian asked through clenched teeth.

Laura looked up at him, hesitantly.

Sebastian eyed her curiously. "What?"

"He's still a director." Whispered Laura.

Sebastian shook his head. "No. You are not talking about Dan Morris, are you?"

Laura nodded.

"He did this to you? I will kill him." Sebastian snarled.

Laura grabbed his arm. "You can't. Just let it go, Sebastian. I've moved on."

"But you haven't. Don't you see? You will not model. You will not act. You were going to walk away from **us**." He looked into her tear filled eyes. "I love you. I do not want to lose you. This does not change the way I feel about you."

"You can't confront Dan about this." Stated Laura.

Sebastian sighed. "You will never get past this if we do not do something."

"Please, Sebastian. It is enough for me that you would even think to do that for me. That you would stand by me. I'm just afraid that if my name is attached to yours, Dan might decide to do something with the tape."

"My only concern about this getting out is how it will affect you emotionally. I know the truth. The people who know you will know the truth. That is the only thing that matters." He rubbed his thumb gently across her cheekbone, wiping away her tears. "I want your name attached to mine. I want to take you out in public. I want people to know who Laura is. They are still talking about you on the boards, you know."

Laura nodded. "I know. Some people think that you're dating one of the cast members in your movie."

Sebastian sighed and sat down. "I never liked Dan before. I have three days left of filming, but this is only the first movie. There are supposed to be several. I don't know if I can work with him."

"This is exactly why I didn't want to tell you. Dan is one of the top directors in the industry. This movie is a big deal to your career. You can't walk away."

Sebastian shook his head. "I couldn't, anyway. I signed a contract for two movies. After that, we will see." He turned to her. "I will not have you near the set, though. I do not want him anywhere near you."

"I do not want to be near him." Commented Laura.

She knelt in front of Sebastian. "You understand now, don't you? This is why we can't see each other anymore."

"No. I understand no such thing." Stated Sebastian. "If you do not want to see me. Fine. But if you are saying that we can't be together because of what happened to you, then I disagree. I love you. It doesn't matter to me about your past. I am in love with this Laura." He laid his hand over her heart. "I am in love with the person in front of me."

Laura sighed. "Sebastian-"

"Do you have another reason why we can't be together?"

Laura shook her head. "No. I love you, too."

"Then we won't have this discussion, again, about your past hurting me." Stated Sebastian.

Laura looked up into his eyes. "You are quite something. You drive me crazy."

"I hope that is a good thing." Sebastian flashed her his lop-sided smile.

"Yes. It is definitely a good thing." Answered Laura.

- - - ☙ - - -

"I miss you." Said Sebastian.

Laura smiled. "I miss you, too." She held the phone to her ear and closed her eyes, lying on her bed. "I'm sure you have plenty to keep you busy."

"I have at least five women a day coming up to me claiming to be Laura. It is a constant reminder of you and how much I miss you."

"You're so sweet. I think about you every day, too."

"You are driving me crazy." Commented Sebastian. "Don't talk like that."

Laura laughed. "Okay. I'll sit up." She sat up and glanced at her picture of Sebastian sitting on her nightstand. "You are so sexy."

"Laura." Sebastian warned his voice a husky timber.

"Okay. Okay. Elizabeth said to tell you hello and she can't wait until you're back this way. Something about me being moody."

Sebastian laughed. "Unfortunately, I do not know when that will be."

"Just take care of yourself."

"I am." Answered Sebastian.

"Good." Laura sighed. "I'm sorry. I've got to go. I have to be in at eight tomorrow and I'm falling asleep on my feet."

"It's okay. I'll talk to you soon."

"I love you. Good night."

"I love you." Answered Sebastian before he hung up.

- - - ∾ - - -

"Laura." Matt walked up to her desk.

"Just one second. Let me write this last message." Laura hung up the phone and turned to Matt. "I was checking voice mail from lunch." She handed him the messages.

"Thank you." He stared at her for a second. "Now. Get out of here and I don't want to see you for at least a week."

Laura stood up abruptly. "Are you firing me?"

Matt laughed. "No. But if you don't take a vacation, I might."

"Am I that bad?" she asked, doubtfully.

"Just go see Sebastian and relax for a while. You've been working too hard." Answered Matt.

"Okay, but for a week? Who's going to run the office?"

"Elizabeth's going to help me out, but I think I can handle most of it."

Laura laughed. "No. Really. Is she working every day?"

"She's going to come in for the afternoons from one to six."

"And you're going to handle everything in the mornings?" asked Laura.

"Yes."

Laura shuddered. "Please promise me that you'll make piles for me and not just throw everything on my desk."

Matt nodded in agreement. "Okay."

"Okay. I'll start my vacation tomorrow. I need to finish up a couple of things first."

"Who's the boss here?" asked Matt, trying not to smile.

Laura smiled sweetly. "You are, but if you want me to come back, you'll let me work for the rest of the afternoon. If it makes you feel any better, I'll call and order my plane ticket right now." Laura reached for the phone.

Matt laughed and started down the hall. "You win, but I don't want to see you the rest of this week or next week."

--- ❧ ---

"So, are you staying busy?" asked Laura.

Sebastian laughed. "You are a comedian. Have you seen the interviews?"

Laura smiled. "Yes. Actually, one is on now." She glanced at her television.

"How many times do you think they are going to replay them?" asked Sebastian.

"I don't know. Probably a lot. Your movie will be coming out soon." Laura pulled two pairs of slacks out of her closet and tossed them onto the bed.

"Yes. There is that." Agreed Sebastian. "Enough about me? How is everything there?"

Laura propped the phone on her shoulder and started packing her clothes into her suitcase. "Same as usual. The editing is in process. So far, it doesn't look like we'll need any reshoots."

"So, will you be getting some time off soon?" asked Sebastian.

"It's too early to tell." Answered Laura, glancing at the clothes she had strewn across her bed.

"I was hoping to see you soon." Hinted Sebastian.

Laura smiled to herself. Won't he be surprised? "I'll let you know as soon as I know something. I miss you, too."

Chapter Nine

The next evening, Laura got off the plane in Los Angeles and walked through the airport to baggage. She had called and spoke to Walter Robertson, Sebastian's agent and flown in to surprise Sebastian. She waited patiently for her luggage and then collected it when it came around on the carousel. She tossed one bag over her shoulder and grabbed the handle of the other one, then proceeded out the doors to catch a taxi. Walter had wanted to send a car, but Laura had refused. She didn't want any fuss. She just wanted to see Sebastian. Things had been good between them since she had told him her deep, dark secret. She had still refused to be seen in public with him, but he was being more patient now that he understood her hesitancy.

Her taxi pulled in front of the hotel and a bellman took her luggage for her. She paid the cab driver and watched him pull away, glancing around at the crowds. Apparently, she wasn't the only one that knew that Sebastian Thomas and the rest of the cast for *Worlds Apart* were staying at this hotel. She followed the bellman into the lobby and then tipped him and took her luggage. She didn't need any help. She knew where she was going. She went to the elevators and got off on the ninth floor. When she stepped off, she noticed a few guards posted around and one stopped her before she could get down the hall.

"Miss? This is a private floor." Said the guard.

Laura nodded. "Yes. Walter Robertson is expecting me." Walter had told her that he would make sure the guards knew that she was coming, so there wouldn't be any problems. Apparently, there had been a communication issue.

The guards exchanged a look. "He's not staying here, ma'am."

Laura sighed. "Of course, he's not. His client, Sebastian Thomas is."

"You're going to have to go back downstairs." Said the second guard.

"Can we just call him? I've had a long flight and I really don't want a lot of people to know that I'm here." Responded Laura.

"And you are?" asked one of the guards.

"Laura Steele." She answered. Like her name would mean anything to them.

The guards exchanged another look. "Are you saying that you are the Mysterious Laura?"

Laura shook her head. "No. I am saying that I am here to see Sebastian. Will you please call Walter?"

Just then another guard stepped off of the elevator. "Is there a problem here?"

"This woman says she's here to see Sebastian or Walter." Answered one of the guards.

"What's your name, ma'am?" asked the guard who had just joined them.

"Laura Steele." She answered.

The man nodded. "Walter said you would be getting here about now. I'm sorry for the misunderstanding. Can I help you with your bags?"

Laura shook her head. "No, thank you." She glanced at the sign showing which numbered rooms were down each hallway. "It's room 913, right?"

"Yes, ma'am."

She smiled at them. "Thank you."

She followed the sign down the hall and around the corner. She passed a few doors and then stopped in front of room 913. What if he wasn't happy to see her? She stared at the door hesitantly for a minute and then took a step back. He had sounded fine last night. She took a deep breath and knocked on the door, then waited for it to open.

"Walter, you-" Sebastian stared at her for a few seconds and then pulled her into his arms. He immediately kissed her and then pulled back. "Are you really here or am I dreaming?"

Laura laughed and glanced down the hall. A couple of the guards were standing at the end watching them. "Let's go inside before we're on the front page."

Sebastian grabbed her suitcase and pulled her inside.

As soon as Sebastian slid her suitcase into the closet, Laura set her shoulder bag in a chair and threw her arms around him and kissed him. "Surprise." She whispered.

"A great one, too." Answered Sebastian, smiling. "When did you plan this?"

"Yesterday. Walter helped me." Said Laura.

"I was wondering why he was so adamant about me being in my room tonight." Said Sebastian.

"Well, it wouldn't have worked if I had to wait in the lobby."

Sebastian laughed. "Did you see all the 'Lauras' down there?"

Laura's eyes widened. "Is that who they are?"

Sebastian nodded. "Yes. They are driving me crazy." He sat on the couch and pulled her down with him. "When are you going to save me?"

Laura touched her hand to his cheek gently. "Soon. I'm just trying to figure out what to do about Dan."

"Damnit. He is here. You can't go anywhere without me."

"I wasn't planning on leaving the room." answered Laura.

"I have an interview in the morning. How long are you here for?" he asked.

"Matt gave me a few days off. How long do you want me?" answered Laura.

Sebastian smiled mischievously. "Hmm. Now that you are here, maybe I will never let you go."

--- ∽ ---

Laura curled up next to Sebastian on the bed and sighed. "I've missed this." She leaned her head on his shoulder and glanced up at him.

He kissed the tip of her nose. "Me, too."

"Did you call the front desk for extra blankets?" asked Laura.

"For what?" asked Sebastian.

"The couch."

"Are you really going to make me sleep on the couch?" asked Sebastian.

Laura smiled at him. "No. I will sleep on the couch."

"Can't we just share the bed?" asked Sebastian. "I promise to behave."

Laura sighed. It wasn't Sebastian that she distrusted. It was herself. Sebastian had been the perfect gentleman. Never pushing for anything.

She, on the other hand, seemed to have things going through her mind daily. Things to do to him. Things to do with him. Her hand tightened on his bicep. His muscled body drove her crazy. They'd never done anything more than kiss, but that was enough to send her body temperature sky high.

She and Sebastian had just hit it off so much better than she could ever have imagined. They never ran out of things to talk about. They had similar tastes but were enough different to make things interesting. Yes. She had fallen hard for him. She just wasn't sure that they were ready for the next step. She didn't want to do anything to jeopardize their relationship. It was so much more than physical. They had proven that, hadn't they?

She glanced over at Sebastian, his t-shirt stretched tautly over his chest. "I guess we can try it for one night." She just hoped that she could survive it.

The next morning, Laura woke to find a note on the pillow beside her.

Laura,

Be back as soon as I can.

Love,

Sebastian

Laura smiled and got up to take a shower. She got dressed and then walked out to the sitting area. There was a note on the table with some fruit and muffins. She smiled. He was always so considerate. She plucked a couple of grapes off of the tray and tossed them into her mouth and then grabbed a glass and looked around for ice. There wasn't any, so she grabbed the bucket and the key card sitting on the table and went out into the hall. She followed the signs to the ice machine and filled up the bucket, then made her way back to the room. She heard the ding of the elevator but didn't look up to see who stepped off.

"Laura?" she heard the familiar voice and stopped. Not him. Anybody, but him. "Laura Steele? What are you doing here?"

Laura glanced up to see Dan Morris standing in front of her. "Dan." She nodded. "Excuse me. I have somewhere to be."

Laura tried to step around him, but Dan moved in front of her. "Were you looking for me?"

Laura bit her lip. "No. Just getting some ice. Excuse me." She tried to get by him, and he moved into her way, again. She sighed and turned around to walk the other way. Dan followed and shoved her up against the wall. Ice flew out of the bucket and scattered like broken glass across the carpet. "Don't walk away from me. I just wanted to talk."

"Dan, just let me go." Responded Laura, trying to keep her voice calm, when she really felt anything but calm.

"I think you were looking for me." He leaned closer to her and pushed his body up against hers. "You want to do another video, don't you?"

Laura flinched, but tightened her grip on the bucket. She just needed him to lean away a little, so she could get her arm free from being wedged against the wall. "Dan, I was not looking for you. Let me go."

Dan laughed. "Who are you here with?"

"That's none of your business."

"Does he know about us? Does he know that you like it rough?" He nuzzled her cheek.

Laura inwardly cringed. She forced herself not to panic. She wasn't the same girl she was six years ago. Dan would not hurt her this time. She heard the elevator again and Dan leaned back from her to look towards the sound. She wrenched her arm free and hit him in the head with the bucket, the remainder of the ice flying into the air, then landing on the floor on the other side of the hall. She jerked free and went running down the hall. Dan caught up to her and shoved her to the floor, knocking the breath out of her. Laura's chin hit the floor and she bit her lip. Dan's weight was pushing her into the carpet. "I remember how this felt. Do you?"

Laura closed her eyes briefly and willed herself not to cry. She forced herself not to think about the last time she was being held down like this. And then he was gone. It took Laura a minute to catch her breath and sit up. She looked up to see Sebastian punch Dan in the nose, and then pull his fist back to punch him, again. She jumped up and grabbed Sebastian's arm.

"Sebastian, no, please." Pleaded Laura.

Sebastian shoved Dan away and watched as he stumbled to the floor.

Then he glanced at Laura. "Are you okay?"

Laura nodded as two of the security guards ran up. She noticed their name tags. John and Sean.

"Where have you guys been?" Snapped Sebastian.

"We had a problem with a group trying to get onto the floor." Said Sean, he glanced at Laura. "Are you okay, ma'am?"

Laura nodded, again and touched her lip. She felt blood trickling down her chin.

John hauled Dan to his feet and looked at Sebastian. "What would you like us to do with him, sir?"

Sebastian looked at Dan who was shooting daggers at him and Laura. "Throw him off of this floor." He looked at Dan.

"Seems you and I have some things to discuss." Dan smirked. "We share the same taste in women."

Sebastian took a step towards him. "You come near her again and you will regret it."

"Did you hear him? He threatened me." Stated Dan.

The guards looked at him and then at Sebastian and Laura. They glanced around the hallway and looked back at Dan. "Actually, I think he was defending himself and his girl." Responded Sean.

John nodded in agreement and pulled Dan down the hall towards the elevators. "Don't worry, sir. He won't get back onto this floor." Said Sean.

"I would appreciate it if this didn't go any further." Said Sebastian, he reached into his pocket, but the guard shook his head.

"Of course not, sir." Said Sean. "Larry was fired this morning for the picture. Generally, we don't have that problem, but he was a new guy and unfortunately, his girlfriend worked for one of the papers."

Sebastian nodded and slipped his arm around Laura. "Thank you." He guided her back to his room and sat her in a chair, then he got a wet washcloth and cleaned her lip, gently. There was a knock on the door, and he strode over to it and swung the door open, prepared to get rid of whoever it was. One of the guards stood there with a bucket of ice. "I thought you might need this, sir. I got another bucket from housekeeping."

"Thank you." Said Sebastian as he accepted the bucket. He closed the door and strode to the bathroom where he grabbed another cloth and wrapped some ice in it, then walked over to Laura. "Here." She took the makeshift cold pack and put it against her lip, wincing.

He sat on the arm of the chair and studied her carefully. "Did he hit you?"

Laura shook her head. "No. He shoved me against the wall. That's all. I'm fine."

"Are you hurt anywhere else?" asked Sebastian, concerned. His eyes traveled slowly over her, inspecting for injuries.

Laura glanced up at him. "No, Sebastian. I'm fine." She leaned back in the chair. "What is this about a picture?"

Sebastian sighed. "One of the guards took a picture of us last night right after you got here. It is in the paper this morning."

"That was quick." Commented Laura. "How clear is the picture?"

"You can't see your face. He took it when I first kissed you. I think he was too scared to take one when we looked down the hall and saw him. So, you are still a mystery." Said Sebastian quietly.

"But you don't want me to be." Guessed Laura.

Sebastian looked down at her. "I am proud of you. You have overcome so much. I want the world to know how special you are."

Laura sighed. "I just don't know, Sebastian."

"Just think about it." Suggested Sebastian.

Laura nodded. "Okay." She stood up. "I'm going to get a shower."

She walked to the bathroom and closed the door, then leaned against it and blew out a long steadying breath. She rushed to the shower and turned on the water, then kicked off her shoes and socks. A sob caught in her throat and she glanced at the door. She didn't want Sebastian to hear her crying. She stepped into the shower and slid to the floor, then let her tears flow freely. Everything flashed before her eyes, the past and the present merging. She pulled her knees to her chest and buried her face in her arms. Would she never be free? She just wanted to move on with her life. Was that too much to ask? Sobs racked her body as the shower soaked her clothes and hair, but still she sat there, not moving, wrapped in her own tormented thoughts.

She hadn't heard him enter the bathroom or open the shower door, but suddenly Sebastian was there wrapping his strong arms around her and holding her while she cried. "I am so sorry, baby. I was hoping to keep you from having to see him at all."

Laura shook her head. "It's not your fault. I should have stayed in the room."

"No. You should be able to go down the hall and get ice if you want." Sebastian sighed and pulled her closer. "Speaking of ice, the water is getting cold."

"I know. I'm sorry." Said Laura.

"Sorry? For what?" Demanded Sebastian. He stood up and pulled her up with him, then turned the water off. He opened the shower door and grabbed a couple towels from the rack beside the shower, then he wrapped her in one and dried her hair with the other one. He stepped out of the shower and grabbed a towel for himself. "I will be right back. Do not move."

Sebastian disappeared and then reappeared with some clothes for her. He spread a towel on the floor and then helped her step out of the shower. "Be careful, please. I will change in the other room." He turned towards the door.

"Sebastian." Said Laura, wanting to see his eyes, again. She could always read his thoughts through his eyes. He turned around and looked at her and she saw everything she needed to. This man loved her, and she was one very lucky woman. "Thank you."

Sebastian smiled at her. "Hurry up. I am hungry." He walked out and pulled the door closed behind him.

Laura smiled and changed into dry clothes, then brushed her hair and went into the bedroom. Sebastian was pulling his shirt down and Laura caught a glimpse of his muscular back. "I figured you'd be finished before me." She commented.

Sebastian smirked at her. "Are you saying that I am slow?"

Laura smiled mischievously and shook her head. "Not slow enough." Sebastian laughed and nodded towards the bed. "Why don't you get comfortable and I will order us some lunch? We can stay in bed all day and watch a movie or something."

Laura smiled and climbed into the bed. "Only if you order from here." She folded back the covers and Sebastian slid in beside her. She snuggled up to him and he slid his arm around her, then picked up the menu from the nightstand.

"What would you like?" he asked, glancing over the menu.

"Anything. I never did get to eat breakfast. Thank you for ordering it for me." Laura sighed as she felt his warmth seep into her. She wouldn't tell Sebastian, but for a few brief moments, she was terrified of what Dan might do to her. She shuddered and closed her eyes, taking a deep breath of Sebastian's familiar spicy scent.

--- ∽ ---

Laura jumped as the wolf leapt out of the bushes. Sebastian chuckled and pulled her closer to him. Laura gasped as the man and the wolf fought, then she glanced at the nightstand. Her phone was vibrating. She sat up and glanced at her phone. Why would Mandy be calling her?

"Hello." Answered Laura.

"Laura, I'm sorry to disturb you. I know this is your time with Sebastian, but I thought you might want to know that the cat is out of the bag." Explained Mandy.

"What do you mean?" asked Laura. Mandy was her best friend from since they were in grade school together. When Laura had gone into modeling, Mandy had gone into journalism.

"You are in Los Angeles with Sebastian, right?"

"Yes. You know I am. I got in last night." Laura could see Sebastian watching her out of the corner of her eye.

"Did you see the photo that came out this morning in the paper?" asked Mandy.

"No. Sebastian said it wasn't clear. That I couldn't be recognized."

"He's right. You can't be recognized by that picture alone, but there was a photographer out front taking pictures when you arrived last night." Sighed Mandy. "And they matched the clothes that you were wearing with the woman in the picture."

"Can you stop it?" begged Laura.

"I'm sorry, Laura. The editor has it. It will be on the front page in the morning." Said Mandy.

Laura glanced at the clock. "Do they have a name?"

"Yes. They found some of your old modeling pictures."

"Does your editor know that you know me?" asked Laura.

"She hasn't remembered that, yet." Answered Mandy.

Laura glanced at Sebastian who looked at her questioningly. "Let me talk to Sebastian and I'll call you back." Laura hung up her phone and turned towards Sebastian. "When's your next premiere?"

"Tomorrow night. Why?" Sebastian eyed her curiously. "That was Mandy?"

Laura nodded. "Yes. It seems the Mysterious Laura is about to be unveiled."

Sebastian frowned. "How?"

"A photographer took my picture out front last night when I got here, and someone matched that photo with the one that the guard took." Explained Laura.

Sebastian nodded in understanding. "What do you want to do?"

"I was thinking- offer Mandy an exclusive interview. Maybe see if her editor will hold off printing it until Friday after the premiere. By then everyone will know if I go with you Thursday night, but Mandy's paper will have the story."

"Do you think her boss will go for it?" asked Sebastian.

"I don't know. It's only one extra day, but my first concern is you. "What do you think?" Laura looked into his eyes, searching for any clue of what he was thinking.

"Laura, Laura." Said Sebastian. "I have wanted to show you off to the world for a while. If you are ready, let's do it."

"Are you sure? What if they dig up my story?" asked Laura. She hadn't realized how important this was to her. Sebastian had said that he wanted the world to know about her and she'd been the one preventing it. It had always seemed to be far off, like something that could happen, but probably never would. So now that it was here, did Sebastian really want everyone to know about her?

Sebastian pulled her close to him. "Honestly, I think that it would hurt Dan's reputation worse than it would hurt yours or mine. Especially, after what the guards witnessed."

He put his finger to her lips when her eyes widened. "Only if any of it comes out. The guards will not say anything unless we ask them to. Do not worry, okay?"

Laura nodded. "Okay. I guess I'll call Mandy, then." Sebastian smiled. "Why don't you invite her for dinner?"

--- ❧ ---

Mandy screamed into the phone when Laura told her what she had planned. "Are you serious?"

"Of course, Mandy. I think you should have the story, but you can only tell what we tell you. Not what you and I have talked about in private." Reminded Laura.

"Of course not, silly. Those are my own Sebastian fantasies lived through you." Mandy laughed. "Let me see what Victoria has to say. Hold on."

Laura heard Mandy knock on a door and then she heard another woman's voice.

"Victoria, would you be interested in an exclusive on the Sebastian Thomas-Laura story?" asked Mandy.

"What do you mean, Amanda?" asked Victoria.

"Sebastian and Laura are offering us an exclusive interview if we will hold the story until Friday after the premiere of *Royalty Unknown*."

"Why?" There was a brief silence. "They are going to go public at the premiere, aren't they?"

"Yes." Answered Mandy.

"When will you do the interview?" asked Victoria. "I am assuming they want you to do the interview."

"Yes, they asked me to do the interview tonight."

"Will they give us a live interview Thursday night?" asked Victoria.

"I will ask them."

"I also want you to take Tony and get photographs." Ordered Victoria.

"Okay. I'll call them to set up a time and let them know that we will hold the story until Friday. Right?"

"Yes. No one else knows about the photographs except you, me and Tony." Answered Victoria. "If they agree to the live interview on Thursday in addition to the one tonight, then we have a deal."

Laura heard a door close and then it was quiet. Then Mandy got back on the phone. "Well, did you hear all of that?" asked Mandy.

"Yes." Laura turned to Sebastian. "Mandy's editor wants a live interview Thursday night at the premiere and some photographs tonight."

"If that is okay with you, then I am fine with it." Sebastian grabbed his phone off of the nightstand. "I need to call Walter and let him know what is going on."

"Hold on, Mandy." Said Laura before she set her phone down and leaned towards Sebastian. "I love you." She whispered and kissed him softly on the mouth.

Sebastian smiled and ran his finger gently down her cheek. "I will do anything you want for that."

Laura laughed and picked up her phone. "That's fine, Mandy. Interview tonight and live interview Thursday." She sighed and added. "And pictures."

"Great. Thanks, Laura. See you guys at 8."

Chapter Ten

$\mathcal{L}$aura hung up the phone. She had called and explained everything to Matt, so that he wouldn't be blindsided if reporters showed up at his place. They both knew it would only be a matter of time. Her life was no longer private. She was dating Sebastian Thomas. The up and coming heartthrob. The guy of many teenagers and women's fantasies. She smiled as she smoothed her lipstick onto her lips.

Sebastian walked up behind her. "What is that smile about?"

Laura turned around into his arms. "Just thinking how lucky I am. I will be envied and hated."

"You call that lucky?" He asked curiously.

Laura laughed. "No. The lucky part is being with you."

Sebastian smiled and kissed her. "I will remind you later that you said that."

"I know you will."

"What did Matt say?"

"He'll be fine. He went through this when I quit modeling. He's going to try to keep Elizabeth away from everything, though. She's not used to dealing with reporters."

There was a knock on the door and Sebastian glanced at Laura. "Ready?"

She took a deep breath and let it out, then nodded. "I'm ready."

Sebastian opened the door to find Mandy and a photographer standing outside. "Come in." Sebastian stepped back and let them enter, then closed the door behind them.

Mandy walked over to Laura and hugged her. "Sorry about dinner. Victoria remembered that we are friends and has added some of her own questions for me to ask. She said that she didn't want our friendship to overshadow my job."

"I'm sorry, Mandy." Replied Laura.

"Don't apologize. Just don't get mad at me. Some of these questions are not my idea."

Laura nodded. "I understand." She glanced at Sebastian and Tony. "Shall we begin?"

"Sure. We're ready when you are." Answered Tony.

Mandy smiled. "Laura, Sebastian, this is our photographer–Tony Reed."

"Nice to meet you, Tony." Laura motioned to the sitting area. "I was thinking that we could just do the interview and pictures right here."

"That will be fine." Agreed Mandy. She followed Laura and Sebastian into the small sitting area of the hotel suite and sat in a chair across from the couch.

Laura sat down across from her and Sebastian sat beside Laura and squeezed her hand in reassurance. Of course, Laura knew if anyone would handle the interview correctly, it would be Mandy. It didn't make it any easier, though.

"Okay." Mandy set her tape recorder in front of her and pulled out a notebook. "Is it okay if I record the interview?"

Laura nodded. "Sure."

"That will be fine, Mandy." Agreed Sebastian.

Mandy smiled at Laura. "Relax. Everything will be fine." Tony stood behind Mandy.

Mandy pressed the record button on the tape recorder. "Let's start with how you two met."

Sebastian smiled and looked adoringly at Laura. "We actually met on-line."

"On-line? How did that happen?" asked Mandy.

"Laura sent me an e-mail and I replied back." Answered Sebastian. "Then we started chatting on-line."

"So, you two hit it off right away?"

"Yes." Agreed Laura. "It was very easy to talk to Sebastian. We talked a lot on-line for several weeks and then met. We've seen each other occasionally since then."

"So, you just decided that you wanted to meet?" asked Mandy.

"Actually, I surprised Laura one day." Said Sebastian.

"Do tell." Prompted Mandy.

"Well, Laura and I started talking about her job and when I found out where she worked, I decided to surprise her in person."

"Why did you decide that?"

"I was curious about the woman that I was talking to on-line. She was intelligent and not intimidated by me at all. She did not gush about who I was. She talked to me like I was a person and I liked that."

Mandy nodded and smiled at him. "So, you like a woman who treats you like an equal and doesn't worship you?"

"Yes."

"You showed up and met her and then you two started dating?"

"Yes. I had decided that she was someone that I wanted to get to know. Meeting her in person was only a formality." Answered Sebastian.

"And you, Laura, what did you think about meeting Sebastian in person?" asked Mandy.

"It was kind of surreal at first. Even though I had been talking to him on-line, I didn't think that I would ever actually meet him." Answered Laura

"And when you did? Was he the same person as on-line?"

"Yes. Even better, if you could believe it. He was not stuck up. He didn't talk down to people or act like he should be treated differently. He acted like a regular person. Only with better manners than some of the people that I've met."

"Sounds like you were impressed by him?" Prodded Mandy.

Laura laughed. "Who wouldn't be? He's Sebastian Thomas. But, then he's just like you and me." Laura looked at Sebastian and smiled. Their eyes caught for a moment.

Tony snapped a couple pictures. Laura glanced at Mandy.

"It's okay." Mandy smiled at her friend. "The only thing that anyone will get out of that shot is how in love you two are." She glanced at Sebastian. "So, how long have you two been seeing each other?"

"About five months." Answered Sebastian.

"Why have you kept it a secret for so long?" asked Mandy as she held up a "V" symbol.

"I wanted to get to know Laura without everyone over our shoulders all of the time." Answered Sebastian.

"What did you think of that?" Mandy asked Laura.

"I agreed. I wanted to spend time with Sebastian as a person, not as the popular heartthrob. I wanted to get to know him, not what everyone else thinks of him."

"Wow. A secret for over five months. So why are you coming out now?" asked Mandy.

"I want Laura to attend events with me. I think it is time for everyone to meet the wonderful woman that I have fallen in love with." Answered Sebastian.

Mandy arched a brow at Laura.

"We're tired of sneaking around." Answered Laura. "If we want to go out to dinner, then we'd like to do that."

Mandy nodded. "How serious are you two?"

"We're not in a rush for anything. We are just enjoying spending time together." Answered Laura.

Mandy nodded at Laura and Sebastian. "Thank you for meeting with me." She turned off the recorder. "I'll need to add something about where you work."

Laura nodded. "I know. I let Matt know what was going on."

"I'm sorry." Said Mandy, sympathetically.

"It's not your fault." Laura glanced at Sebastian. "I knew what I was getting into. I knew eventually if we were together long enough, then my life would become public knowledge."

"I think the interview went great." Said Mandy. "I'll work on it tonight and submit it to Victoria tomorrow morning. I can get you a copy probably by the evening."

"Sounds good." Answered Laura.

"Now if you two will just relax a little on the couch, then I'll get a couple shots and we'll be out of your way." Said Tony.

Laura and Sebastian leaned back on the couch and Sebastian put his arm around her shoulders. They both smiled. Tony snapped a couple pictures and then Laura leaned against Sebastian and Tony took a couple more. He smiled at them. "You two take great pictures. You're both so photogenic."

"Which reminds me." Commented Mandy. "Victoria wants a little blurb put in about your past work as a model."

Laura nodded. "Of course, she does." She smiled at her friend. "No problem. Thanks for handling everything."

"Thank you for the story." Replied Mandy. She hugged her friend and then followed Tony to the door.

"Thank you, Mandy. Thank you, Tony." Said Sebastian as he saw them to the door. He closed the door behind them and then turned to Laura. "That wasn't so bad, was it?"

Laura shook her head. "No, but it is just the beginning."

--- ❧ ---

Laura slid under the covers and curled up next to Sebastian. "You're such a gentleman. Sleeping in the same bed with me and not making any moves." Commented Laura.

Sebastian smiled. "You would not say that if you knew what was going through my mind."

Laura slid her hand slowly up Sebastian's chest in a gentle caress. "Why don't you show me?"

Sebastian glanced at Laura. "Do not tease me."

Laura looked up at him through her eyelashes and angled herself, so she was lying partially across his body. "I'm not teasing." She leaned up and ran her tongue across his lips. He opened his mouth and caught her tongue between his lips, then kissed her gently, taking control.

Sebastian flipped her onto her back and leaned over her. "Are you sure?"

"I'm sure." Laura answered, breathlessly. "I want you to make love to me, Sebastian."

Sebastian studied her for a moment, then nodded, seeming to find whatever he was looking for. "Your wish is my command." He leaned down and took possession of her mouth.

Laura's hands slid under Sebastian's t-shirt and up his back, gliding over his muscles, feeling them bunch and flex under her fingers while Sebastian's hands gently stroked and explored her body. She felt her body temperature rising, her skin getting heated from his touch.

She wanted to feel his hands everywhere.

Sebastian's kisses moved to her neck and shoulders, then trailed downward over her breasts and to her stomach. Laura pulled Sebastian's shirt over his head and ran her hands up his chest and shoulders and into his hair where she gripped a handful gently and pulled Sebastian's mouth back to hers. "You are driving me crazy." She whispered.

"The night has just started." Sebastian promised.

Chapter Eleven

aura rolled over and stretched. The bed was cold beside her. She opened her eyes and sat up as Sebastian walked into the bedroom with a tray.

"Good morning, sleepy head." He leaned over to kiss her, and Laura looked down. She slipped her hand in front of her mouth and glanced back up. "I need to brush my teeth."

Sebastian laughed and kissed her hand. "After you eat." He set a tray of food in front of her and pulled the cover off the dish sitting in the center of the tray.

"I can't eat all of this food." exclaimed Laura, eyeing the eggs, bacon, muffins and fruit in front of her.

Sebastian smiled. "I'll share with you."

"Are you trying to spoil me?"

"You deserve to be spoiled." Sebastian answered.

Laura drank a sip of her juice. "What are the plans for today?" She grabbed a fork and started eating some of the scrambled eggs.

"I need to run a few errands and then I thought I could meet you back here for lunch."

"I need to go shop for a dress for tonight." Said Laura as she grabbed half of a muffin off the tray and started eating it.

She plucked a couple of strawberries off of the plate.

Sebastian smiled. "After lunch."

"You're not giving me much time." Laura sat back from the tray. "I'm stuffed. I can't eat any more."

Sebastian picked up the tray. "Why don't you go ahead and get a shower? I am not leaving, yet."

Laura nodded. "Okay. Be out in a minute."

--- ❧ ---

"I will be by in about thirty minutes to pick it up. Do not sell it to anyone else." Said Sebastian. He closed his cell phone and glanced at the bathroom door. The shower was still running. He moved over to the closet and glanced at some of the size tags on Laura's clothes. Good. The size was right.

He heard the shower turn off and quickly sat at the table in the sitting room and opened the newspaper, then glanced at his watch. Laura exited the bathroom in a fuzzy white robe. Sebastian's gaze traveled slowly over her and smiled.

"Something amusing?" asked Laura.

Sebastian shook his head. "No. I was just thinking."

"About?"

"Should I describe last night's activities?" Sebastian flashed her his one-sided smile, as he watched her cheeks redden.

"Behave yourself." Laura scolded playfully, as she walked over to the closet, and someone knocked on the door. Sebastian answered it and a woman stepped into the room. "Laura, this is Rachel. She is a masseuse. She is here for you for the next hour and a half. Rachel, this is Laura."

Laura turned around in surprise. "For me?"

Sebastian smiled and kissed her quickly on the mouth. "Yes. For you. I will be back shortly. Relax and enjoy." Sebastian left the room, quietly closing the door behind him.

--- ∽ ---

Laura glanced at the tall, slender blonde. "Hello."

Rachel smiled at her. "I'll just set up my table over here if that's okay."

"Sure." Laura glanced at the robe that she was wearing. "I haven't had a chance to get dressed, yet."

"That's not necessary. It would be better if you didn't." answered Rachel as she put sheets on the table.

Laura nodded, a little unsure. "Okay."

Rachel set a small portable radio/cd player on a nearby table and turned it on. Soft soothing music flowed into the room. "Okay. I'm ready when you are."

Laura smiled faintly and walked over to the table.

"Lay on your stomach and put your face on this cushion." Instructed Rachel, indicating which way she should lay down.

Laura followed her directions and took a deep breath as she slid onto the table. She slid her robe off and was glad that she at least had underwear on. Rachel placed a sheet over her lower body. She heard Rachel open a bottle and rub her hands together, then felt her slick hands on her back. She started to relax as she felt Rachel's hands knead her tense muscles.

"If you want, I'll be quiet." Said Rachel. "I wanted to ask you a question, though."

"Sure." Answered Laura.

"How long have you been dating Sebastian?"

Laura smiled. "Five months on Friday."

"He's a good guy." Responded Rachel.

"Yes, he is. How long have you known him?" asked Laura.

"Two years." Answered Rachel. "He's one of my regular clients."

"I can see why. This feels wonderful." Purred Laura.

"My job is to please." Smiled Rachel. "What happened to your face?"

Laura tensed. "I hit a wall."

"I know Sebastian didn't do that." stated Rachel.

"No. Sebastian wouldn't do something like this." Answered Laura.

"Sebastian said that he's taking you to the premiere tonight." Commented Rachel.

"Yes. It will be our first public appearance."

"Are you going to the spa this afternoon?" asked Rachel.

"No. I have to go and get a dress. I hadn't planned for the premiere."

"If you get an appointment for two, they could do your hair, makeup, nails, probably all in two hours. You could shop for a dress beforehand." Offered Rachel.

"Maybe. They probably could do a better job at covering the bruise on my face."

"Yes. The ladies are good down there. They all adore Sebastian, too."

Laura smiled. "I don't know anyone who doesn't."

After a long tranquil ninety minutes of Rachel working all of the tightness and stress out of her muscles, Laura sat up on the table and slipped her robe back on. She felt like she was going to sink into a puddle on the floor, she was so relaxed.

Rachel walked back into the room from the sink with her phone to her ear. "Yes. Two o'clock for Laura Steele. Thank you, Cammie. Bye." She closed her phone. "You're all set."

"Thank you." Laura moved to the chair in the room and watched as Rachel started folding up the table.

Sebastian walked into the room. "Hello ladies."

He smiled at Laura. "How was your massage?"

"Wonderful. Thank you."

Sebastian hung two clothing bags on the closet door. "Ready for lunch?"

Laura sighed. "I need to get dressed and go shop for a dress."

Sebastian smiled and turned back towards the closet. He unzipped one of the bags. "How about this one?" He pulled a hunter green floor length satin dress with spaghetti straps, an open back and a cinched waist out of the bag.

"You picked this out for me?" asked Laura, walking over to the dress. She looked up at Sebastian whose eyes showed a little doubt on whether he had done the right thing.

"Do you like it?"

"It's beautiful." She breathed.

"The sales lady picked out a pair of shoes. I hope they are okay." He pulled the box out of the bottom of the bag. Laura opened the box and looked at the shoes. She pulled the matching shoes out of the box and slipped them onto her feet. They fit perfectly. "You checked my sizes."

"Guilty." Replied Sebastian.

Laura threw her arms around his neck. "You are amazing." She kissed him. Sebastian put his hands on her waist and pulled her closer, deepening the kiss.

Rachel cleared her throat. "I'll just be going. I'll see you later, Laura."

Laura pulled back from Sebastian, embarrassed. "I'm sorry, Rachel."

Rachel smiled at the two of them. "No problem. It's nice to see Sebastian happy. It was nice to meet you, Laura."

"Nice to meet you, too, Rachel. Thank you."

"Thank you, Rachel." Said Sebastian.

"You're welcome. You were right. She needed it. See you later." Rachel closed the door behind her.

Laura giggled. "I can't believe you made me forget she was here."

Sebastian smiled. "I am just glad you like the dress."

"That was so thoughtful of you."

"I didn't want you to worry about anything for tonight."

"Thank you." Laura touched the dress that was now hanging on the closet door.

"Want some lunch?" asked Sebastian.

"We just had breakfast two hours ago."

"I know, but it will be another hour before it gets here, and we will not eat until late tonight."

"Okay. Do they have a grilled chicken salad?"

"I think so." Sebastian grabbed the menu from the table and sat on the edge of the bed. He picked up the phone and called down to the restaurant to place their order. Laura hiked up her robe and climbed onto Sebastian's lap, straddling him. He raised an eyebrow at her and confirmed their order, then hung up.

"What are you doing?" he asked.

Laura smiled sweetly. "Sitting on your lap."

"I could not tell." He said, amusement dancing in his eyes.

Laura ran her finger over Sebastian's lips and watched as he sucked her finger into his mouth. She felt the heat uncurling in her stomach and briefly closed her eyes. She slipped her hands to his chest and shoved him back onto the bed, following him down. Her mouth covered his and her tongue slid inside to tease him. She felt his hands run up her back and into her hair where they stopped and held her head in place while his tongue invaded her mouth.

When they pulled breathlessly apart, Laura sat up and moved her hands to the belt of her robe. She slowly untied it and slid open her robe, letting it fall off of her shoulders.

Sebastian looked up at Laura sitting astride him. She was the most beautiful woman he had ever seen. Her long red hair fell over her delicate shoulders. His gaze traveled over her bare flesh, tracing every curve and shape of her body and then stopping at the scrap of blue lace that was the only piece of clothing she wore. His fingers gently, slowly followed the trail that his gaze had gone and briefly halted at the band at her hips, then slowly slid underneath. He traced the band forward to her stomach and watched as her skin quivered at his touch. He looked up into her green eyes, darkened with desire and held her gaze, then slid his fingers further down under the lace. Her body trembled and he felt rather than heard her intake of breath.

Laura stared into Sebastian's deep blue eyes and felt like she was on fire. Her body burned everywhere he had touched. Her body trembled, waited, almost impatiently for the next touch. She felt his fingers sliding down her flesh.

Laura jumped at the knock on the door. "Room service." She groaned in displeasure and fell to the side onto the bed and pulled her robe closed.

Sebastian sighed and ran his hands through his hair. He glanced at the clock. Lunch only took thirty minutes today. He leaned over and kissed Laura, then stood up and took a deep breath and walked over to the hall door, pulling the bedroom door closed behind him.

Laura sighed and grabbed some clothes and got dressed. She couldn't muster one ounce of regret for taking their relationship to the next level. Now that she had a taste, though, she wanted so much more. She walked out of the bedroom to find Sebastian on the phone.

"Sorry, Walter. We promised the interview to *LA Info*." Sebastian paced across the floor. "They will just have to wait. I have interviews lined up for next week. You know that….. No, not for this. For *Worlds Apart*….. Yes, I imagine there will be questions about Laura, too…I am not doing interviews the whole time that Laura is here….. Okay,

Walter. I will talk to them tomorrow…. No, I am not promising Laura. Bye." Sebastian hung up.

"What's wrong?" asked Laura.

Sebastian turned to look at her. "Nothing."

Laura walked over to Sebastian and put her hand on his cheek. "Tell me."

Sebastian sighed. "Walter wants to set up an interview with another magazine for tomorrow. It seems that the picture in the paper has brought up more questions about the mysterious Laura."

"I'll go with you tomorrow."

"Let's see how you feel after tonight, okay?" He covered her hand with his. "Besides, I don't want to share you the whole time that you are here."

--- ☙ ---

Laura felt like a princess as she made her way back up to the room. She had been pampered all afternoon. All of the women knew that she was with Sebastian and talked about how gorgeous and nice he was and how lucky she was. She sighed, wondering how much info would get leaked before tonight. She stepped off of the elevator and passed two of the security guards for the floor. She nodded and smiled.

"Do you believe what Bobby said about the other day?" one of them whispered.

"What do you mean?"

"Do you think she was really attacked or just caught in the act?"

"You mean the situation with the director?" she heard some shuffling. "Don't talk about that. You are being disrespectful."

Laura hurried down the hall to Sebastian's room and then stepped inside and closed the door. She leaned against it for a minute and took a deep breath. It hadn't taken long for the talk to start. How long before the story was out? The whole story? The real story or one pieced together by assumptions and gossip?

Laura watched Sebastian move around the bedroom. He was wearing his black tuxedo slacks and sliding into his shirt. She took advantage of the moment to admire his well-honed body. His muscled biceps and flat, hard stomach. His broad shoulders and chest. She sighed, remembering what that body felt like naked against hers. Sebastian turned around and saw her.

"There you are. How was your afternoon?" he walked over to her, buttoning his shirt.

Laura forced a bright smile. She didn't want him to know about the guards. He didn't need to worry about that along with everything else. Tonight, was to celebrate him.

"Great! All the women are your fans."

He kissed her gently. "Were they nice?"

Laura smiled. "Very nice." She walked over to the closet and unzipped the bag with her dress inside, then slid off her jeans and t-shirt.

"I am glad you enjoyed yourself." He watched as she stepped into her dress, then zipped it up for her. She put her shoes on and went into the bathroom to put in her earrings, then brought her necklace to Sebastian. He put it around her neck and clasped it, then nuzzled her neck and kissed it. "I like your hair up."

"Thank you, handsome." Replied Laura. She turned around and stepped into his arms.

Sebastian held her a moment and then pulled back. "You okay?"

Laura nodded. "Just a little nervous. I'm fine. I'm excited to see your movie."

"I'll take a nap. You can wake me when it is over."

"You will not." Laura laughed as she nudged his hands aside and adjusted his bow tie for him.

"I never watch my movies. This will be a first." Answered Sebastian.

"Then what do you usually do at these premieres?"

"Show up, visit with the fans, talk to friends, media and cast members, then leave."

"We could do that tonight."

Sebastian shook his head. "No. I know you want to see this movie. Besides, I can't disappoint my biggest fan."

"I'm much more than just a fan."

"Yes, you are." Agreed Sebastian as he leaned down to kiss her.

--- ❧ ---

"Have I told you how beautiful you are?" Sebastian turned to Laura and placed his hand against her cheek.

"Yes. Thank you." Laura smiled. They were sitting in the back of a limousine, on their way to the movie premiere in Hollywood at the *El Capitan Theatre.* The traffic was slowing as they got closer to the theatre. Fans were lined up outside, hoping for a glimpse of their favorite actor or actress. Cars would pull up to the red carpet and the actors, actresses, directors and other celebrities would step out onto the red carpet amongst screams and shouts from their fans.

Laura glanced around at the people lining the streets and walkways.

Sebastian glanced at her and smiled. "You ready?"

"Are you sure you want to do this?" asked Laura, looking out the window. She wasn't sure. What if the fans hated her? What if her secret hurt Sebastian's career?

"Laura." Sebastian grabbed her hand and tugged to get her attention. She turned towards him, and he slanted his mouth over hers and took possession, deepening the kiss and caressing her neck with his other hand. When he was sure he got his message across to her, he pulled away and leaned his forehead against hers. "I love you."

Laura forced a smile. She was still unsure about their decision, but she did love this man. "I love you, too."

"My fans will love you, too."

Laura laughed. "I wouldn't go that far." She readied herself as their car pulled to a stop and Sebastian sat forward. "Sebastian." She grabbed his arm.

"Yeah?" he glanced back at her.

"Don't worry about me. Take care of your fans. Okay?"

Sebastian smiled at her. "I will not leave your side."

The limo door was opened, and Sebastian stepped out. There were fans lined up to his right, screaming and yelling his name. Sebastian turned and smiled and waved to them. Cameras flashed and he blinked, then he turned back towards the car and offered his hand to help Laura out of the car. Later, he would swear that it went silent, but no one else remembered it that way. Laura stepped out of the car and the noise grew louder.

The Media lined the left side of the aisle and there were microphones and recorders shoved in their direction. He vaguely heard questions, but Sebastian just smiled and moved to the right side to sign autographs and touch hands. He smiled for pictures and said hello to fans and always kept Laura by his side.

Finally, they made their way to the end of the aisle and *LA Info* was waiting. Mandy smiled reassuringly at Laura, then turned towards the cameraman beside them. "I am Amanda Knight with *LA Info* at the premiere of *Royalty Unknown*. We are here with Sebastian Thomas, and it seems that we might get an answer to the long-asked question 'Who is the Mysterious Laura?'"

She turned to Sebastian and Laura. "Sebastian, it's nice to see you." Smiled Amanda. "Is it okay if I ask you a few questions?"

Sebastian smiled. "Sure." He squeezed Laura's hand.

"Is this lovely lady beside you the Laura that everyone has been wondering about?"

"Yes. This is Laura." Confirmed Sebastian. "The one that everyone has been curious about."

"This is your first public appearance, isn't it?" asked Amanda.

"Yes." Answered Sebastian.

"How long have you been seeing each other and why did you wait so long to go public?"

"We have been seeing each other for several months and we have been spending our time getting to know each other." Sebastian gave his famous one-sided smile. "Honestly, Amanda, I like to keep my personal life personal."

"I can understand that, but your fans would like to know if you're single or not."

Sebastian laughed. "I am definitely not single."

"Do I detect something more permanent in that comment?" asked Amanda.

"Personal life personal, Amanda." Commented Sebastian. He winked at her. "If there is anything to report, I will let you know."

Amanda smiled and turned towards Laura. "How does it feel to be dating one of the biggest heartthrobs in the industry?"

Laura smiled and glanced at Sebastian. "As popular as he is, to me, he is just Sebastian the person, not Sebastian the actor."

"Well, there you have it ladies. Sebastian's Laura." Amanda turned back to them. "Thank you very much for your time. Enjoy your movie."

"Thank you." Responded Sebastian. He slipped his arm around Laura, and they walked into the building.

Laura glanced around the lobby, taking in the intricate designs and the people everywhere. Actors, actresses, models, directors. Names she'd heard and seen on billboards, in newspapers, magazines, movie credits, on the entertainment channel. She tried not to be overwhelmed and took a breath. This had almost been her life. She shook her head. Not going there, especially tonight.

--- ❦ ---

Sebastian saw his friend, Jason, walking towards them as he and Laura stepped into the lobby.

"You really know how to stir up a crowd." Jason commented as he stopped next to them and clapped Sebastian on the back. He turned to Laura and held out his hand.

"I'm Jason Black."

Laura smiled and shook his hand. "Nice to meet you. I'm–

"The mysterious Laura." Interrupted Jason.

Laura laughed. "That's me. Mysterious."

"Jason Black Laura Steele." Introduced Sebastian.

Jason studied her, curiously. "**The** Laura Steele?"

Laura looked at him questioningly. "I'm sure there's another one somewhere."

Jason shook his head. "Weren't you in the movie '*Raven's Prey*?"

Sebastian watched the emotions play across Laura's face. Shock, surprise… dread.

Jason nodded, answering his own question. "It is you. Where have you been? I thought I'd be hearing your name all over the place after that?"

Laura shook her head. "No. That wasn't my thing. I'm an agent assistant."

Jason laughed and then stopped abruptly when he noticed her and Sebastian's expressions. "You're serious."

Sebastian placed his hand at Laura's waist. "Laura works at *Studio B.*"

Sebastian watched as his friend started to ask a question, then changed his mind. "It's nice to finally meet you." offered Jason.

"Thank you." Replied Laura, relief briefly flashing across her face.

- - - ∽ - - -

Laura stood in front of the mirror in the ladies room. She shouldn't be surprised that someone would recognize her from her earlier career. She couldn't hide forever. Of course, it would have to be Sebastian's best friend, Jason Black. What were the chances? He had starred in '*Raven's Prey*', also. She remembered that he had been really nice. He'd been just starting out, too. Now you saw his name everywhere. Along with Sebastian's.

She sighed. She didn't think that Jason had been connected to '*Lover's Secret*', but he could have been. She touched up her lipstick and checked her hair and make-up in the mirror. She was a different woman now. Definitely not naïve and innocent like six years ago. Yes, she was strong enough to stand by Sebastian. Was their relationship really strong enough to stand up to what was to come?

She knew that Dan wouldn't let it go. Not after the incident at the hotel. He needed to dominate people and she had fought him. Sebastian had intervened. No, Dan wasn't finished with her. Laura took a deep breath. Enough of that type of thought. Tonight, was about Sebastian.

--- ღ ---

Sebastian watched Laura walk across the room and smiled. Heads turned as she passed; eyes followed her. She didn't realize how beautiful she was- inside and out. She was always so concerned with everyone else before herself. Even when it was herself that she should be worried about. That was his Laura. Yes, *his* Laura. He watched her smile and speak briefly to someone who had stopped her. She nodded and her eyes caught his. He saw genuine laughter there and was relieved to see that she was enjoying herself.

Jason stopped beside him. "She's something."

"Yes. She is." Sebastian agreed. He felt his friend studying him. "What?"

"Be careful. There's a reason that she's been out of the spotlight for six years."

Sebastian nodded. "I know."

"You know there's a reason or you know the reason?" asked Jason.

"Both." Answered Sebastian.

Jason nodded. "Good. I would hate for there to be secrets between you and the woman you love."

"We do not have secrets."

The two men watched her walk up to them.

"Ready for the movie?" asked Sebastian as he offered his arm to Laura.

"Yes." Laura placed her hand into the crook of his arm. "This will be a new experience. Sitting beside you while watching one of your movies." Laura smiled up at him. "I don't know which I'll be watching more of."

Sebastian laughed and pulled her close. "I don't want to distract you. Should I find another seat?"

"No." answered Laura. "I think I can concentrate. After all, I have you later." They stared into each other's eyes.

"Maybe I should find another seat." Commented Jason, dryly.

Laura smiled at him. "Don't worry. We can control ourselves."

--- ⁀ ---

"You never told me that you could sing." Accused Laura, who was walking between Sebastian and Jason as they left the theatre.

"It's just a hobby." Answered Sebastian.

Laura glanced up at him. "It should be much more. You have a great voice."

Sebastian smiled at her. "Thank you."

"Mr. Thomas. Mr. Black." Said a man approaching them.

"Yes?" answered Sebastian, turning towards the voice. He smiled. "Hello Mike."

"Mr. Robertson sent us." Answered Mike as he motioned to the three other men with him. "It seems you and Ms. Steele have gotten a lot of attention tonight."

Sebastian nodded. "That was thoughtful of Walter, but we are just going back to the hotel tonight."

Mike nodded. "We'll see you to the hotel." He stepped in front of them and motioned his men into position, as they escorted them to the awaiting limousine.

"Let's get together while we're both in town." Said Jason.

"Sounds good. Call me." Agreed Sebastian.

Jason nodded and slipped away.

- - - ♧ - - -

Laura glanced out the window while they pulled up to the hotel. People were scattered everywhere and began cheering when they saw their car. The bodyguards surrounded her and Sebastian as they entered the hotel and rode with them up the elevator. They escorted them to their room and then left after they were inside.

Sebastian turned to Laura after he closed the door. "I have you to myself at last."

Laura looked up at him and smiled. "Now that you have me, what are you going to do with me?"

Sebastian smiled mischievously and scooped her up into his arms, then carried her to the bedroom. "I shall show you."

Chapter Twelve

aura sat at the table, eating breakfast when someone knocked on the hotel door. She answered it and received copies of the newspaper and the *LA Info* for the week. There was a snapshot of her and Sebastian on the front. She flipped it open to the article and sat back down to read it. Mandy had sent over a copy of the article, but with everything going on, she'd only had time to scan it. The caption read:

LA Info

Meet Sebastian Thomas and the Mysterious Laura

by Amanda Knight

Photography by Anthony Reed

By now, everyone has heard of the mysterious Laura, but no one has met her. Last night, Sebastian and Laura made their first appearance at the premiere of the much-anticipated movie Royalty Unknown. I had the opportunity to sit down with them and chat.

Sebastian and Laura have been seeing each other secretly for five months and have spent as much time as possible while both have been filming movies. Sebastian was filming his next movie Worlds Apart, which comes out fall of next year and Laura was filming Dawn's Cover which doesn't have a release date, yet. Which brings us to the next question. How did they meet?

Sebastian and Laura met on-line. Laura sent Sebastian a message (See, ladies, they do read their fan mail.) and Sebastian responded. After talking on-line for a couple weeks, Sebastian wanted to meet Laura. So, he flew to meet her. He showed up with flowers and took her to dinner. Ever since then, they've been inseparable. They've stayed out of the spotlight, so they could get to know each other, but are tired of hiding and want to be able to go out places. While this journalist is sad to see Sebastian Thomas taken off of the singles list, it is nice to see him happy. Yes, ladies, he is happy and in love. Just check out the pictures taken of the two of them together.

I know what you're still asking. Who is the mysterious Laura?

Her name is Laura Steele, and she lives in Savannah, Georgia. This should explain the lack of sightings of Sebastian Thomas while filming in Hilton Head, South Carolina. The two locations are about an hour apart. Laura currently works for Matt Logan at Studio B, a talent agency that handles various talent including models, actors, actresses, etc. and yes, they have just produced a movie. Matt Logan started the agency fifteen years ago and has produced five movies so far. Laura Steele was and is one of his talents. She was a model for several years and has had small parts in a couple of movies, but decided she enjoyed the behind the scenes work better.

So far, I haven't heard that there will be any changes in her career. Sebastian and Laura will be seeing each other as much as they can around their busy work schedules.

They were both very gracious and happy to answer my questions. They seem to be very happy together and I'm sure we will be seeing much more of them in the future.

- - - ∽ - - -

Sebastian stepped out of the bathroom and Laura glanced up from the article. Sebastian had a towel wrapped around his waist and was bare-chested. Water glistened off of his chest and shoulders. Laura swallowed and let her eyes travel the length of his body, then back up to his face. Sebastian's eyes darkened and he walked towards her. "Baby, if you keep looking at me like that, we will not make it to the interview on time."

Laura smiled and stood up. "Interview?"

Sebastian reached out and grabbed her arm and pulled her against his chest, his mouth hovered above hers. "What interview, indeed." He whispered, then lowered his mouth over hers. He drank Laura like she was water and he'd been lost in the desert, dehydrated and thirsty for days. She drove him crazy. Now that they had gotten closer, it was impossible to be away from her. Thoughts of doing anything but having her in his arms were unimportant.

The phone rang and he reluctantly pulled back from her, he leaned his forehead against hers and breathed heavily. "You drive me out of my mind." He whispered, then turned from her and strode to the nightstand to answer the phone.

Laura watched Sebastian walk away and took a deep breath to steady herself. Their physical attraction hadn't wavered at all since their relationship had changed. It seemed to only get stronger. As a matter of fact, nothing had changed. They still had tons of things to talk about. There was no awkwardness or uncomfortable moments. They still spent as much time together as possible. She still got that feeling when he walked into the room. The one where she couldn't catch her breath and was excited to see him. She still wanted to be near him and thought about him all the time.

Sometimes, though, she wondered why he wanted to be with her. Things would be so much easier for him if he dated someone else. Would Dan actually leave her alone or would he try to cause problems for them? She walked over to the closet as Sebastian hung up the phone.

"That was Walter. He's sending a car for us. It will be here in about fifteen minutes." Sebastian told her.

Laura sighed. Some things had changed. Now the public knew. She pulled a pair of slacks and a blouse out of the closet and slipped into them, then went into the bathroom to apply her makeup. She hoped that she had done the right thing, staying with Sebastian. She loved him. She just hoped that Dan would back off and stay out of their life.

--- ✺ ---

"Mandy, please, meet us tonight." Pleaded Laura.

Mandy laughed into the phone. "If you don't let me get off the phone, I'll never finish this article and I won't be able to come."

"Okay. Meet us at seven at *The Cabana Club.*" Laura said quickly and hung up.

Laura turned to Sebastian. "She'll be there."

"I am not sure that you should be doing this." Said Sebastian as he leaned down and kissed Laura on the lips.

"I'm not doing anything. We're just meeting two of our friends to have a good time." Replied Laura, slipping her arms around Sebastian's neck and tugging him down for another kiss.

Sebastian smiled, knowingly. "Of course."

--- ✺ ---

Laura hugged her friend. "I'm so glad you came. Let's get a table."

"Where's Sebastian?" asked Mandy, as she glanced around the club.

"He'll be right in. He's meeting someone." Answered Laura.

Mandy grabbed her friend's arm. "You are not setting me up." The words were more an accusation than a question.

"Why would you think that?" asked Laura as she slid into a seat at the first available empty table she saw.

Mandy sat beside her. "You wouldn't do something like that. I would."

Laura nodded. "You're right. You would." Her eyes scanned the crowd, looking for a waitress.

"Amanda Knight?"

The women turned as they heard her name. Mandy grabbed Laura's arm and pulled her closer. "Hide me."

"Too late. He's already seen you. Who is he anyway?" asked Laura curiously, glancing over Mandy's shoulder at the dark-haired man making his way towards them.

"Do you remember my date from hell?" hissed Mandy.

"Oh, no." gasped Laura as she glanced around for Sebastian.

"Amanda. It is you." The guy stopped beside the table and stuck his face into Mandy's. "Where have you been? I tried to call you a couple times."

The guy kept talking like he'd been answered, and they were having a conversation. "I thought our date was great and we could get together, again. I'm single. You're single. We had great chemistry." The guy slurped his drink.

Amanda sunk further into her chair. "I'm not single, Brad."

"I don't see anyone here except your friend here." Brad sat down across from them and leaned over the table. "We need some drinks over here!"

Laura glanced around and saw Sebastian heading towards them with Jason beside him. She sent him a desperate look. He looked at her questioningly and then narrowed his gaze on Brad.

- - - ∽ - - -

"I can't believe you guys are trying to set me up. Not only are you doing that, but you're trying to set me up with Amanda Knight." Grumbled Jason.

"Mandy is Laura's best friend. Quit complaining and help me deal with this situation. Laura is sending me looks of desperation." Answered Sebastian.

Jason's eyes strayed to the women. "I can see why. Mr. Cool is drunk and rowdy."

"Amanda, you know we'd be great, right? Wasn't our date awesome?" asked Brad.

Mandy shook her head and tried to pull her hand out of Brad's grasp. "Brad. We can't see each other, anymore."

"Sure we can." Brad responded not even listening to Mandy. He just smiled at her.

"Mandy, baby. Sorry I'm late. Who's your friend?" asked Jason as he stepped up beside her and slid his arm around her waist.

Brad jerked his hand back. "You been cheating on me, Amanda."

Mandy shook her head. "I told you that I wasn't single. I met Jason after our date."

"I thought that night meant something. You–"

"I wouldn't say anything else, buddy. Just get up and walk away." Interrupted Jason.

Brad looked at Jason and then glanced at Sebastian, who had stepped up to the other side of the table and beside Laura.

"Alright man." Brad stood up and staggered away.

"Want to tell us what that was all about?" asked Jason.

"Thank you." Answered Mandy in relief.

Laura giggled and everyone looked at her. "I'm sorry. The situation isn't funny. I was just remembering what Mandy had told me about that guy."

"Do tell. We would all like to enjoy the joke." Commented Jason, dryly.

"Shall I do introductions?" offered Laura.

"Not necessary." Answered Jason and Mandy, simultaneously. Laura glanced at Sebastian, who squeezed her hand.

"So, we're sitting in this fine restaurant and he sucks the last drop of liquid from his glass, slurping loudly and then raises it into the air and shouts 'Refill!'". Mandy shakes her head. "I thought I was going to die on the spot. He's got ketchup on his chin because he insisted on ordering a burger and loaded it with all the condiments."

Laura's laughing so hard, tears are sliding down her cheeks, Sebastian and Jason can't stop laughing and the waitress drops off their drinks, handing a pile of napkins to Laura and laughing as she leaves the table.

"The date from hell." Said Jason.

Mandy nods. "Yes. I thought he gave up until tonight."

Jason glanced at her. "Maybe he will now that he's seen you with someone else."

"I hope so. Thanks, again."

"No problem. I don't like to see a damsel in distress" Answered Jason.

Mandy smiled at him. "I appreciate that."

"So, tell me. How do you two know each other? You are on opposite sides of the map." asked Jason.

"We grew up together." Answered Mandy. "Went to school together and kept in touch."

Laura nodded and sipped her drink. "Yes. We talk every week."

"I still don't understand why you chose to be in Savannah, Georgia. Your best friend is in LA, and you obviously had a promising career." Prodded Jason.

Laura swallowed and looked Jason in the eyes. "I realized after doing a couple of movies, that I was more comfortable behind the scenes than in them."

Jason studied her. "Really? That's strange. Usually people love to be in the spotlight."

Laura shook her head. "No. I'm happy working at *Studio B*."

"You must like it some. You are dating Sebastian."

"If I had a choice, no one would know that I was dating Sebastian Thomas." Answered Laura. "As much as I love being with him, I don't like sharing my life with the world."

"I-" Jason began but was interrupted.

"Enough interrogating my girlfriend." Said Sebastian. He got up from the table and pulled Laura onto the dance floor.

Jason watched them briefly, then turned his attention to Mandy. "You know, don't you?" he shook his head when she tried to respond. "I know you won't tell me, but just know that I won't stand for my friend getting hurt."

Mandy frowned at him. "Sebastian knows everything. You need to let it go. Let them be happy."

"I will until it starts affecting Sebastian or his career, then I'll be right in the middle of it."

Jason and Mandy stared at each other, sizing up one another as Sebastian and Laura danced together on the dance floor, oblivious to their friends' standoff.

--- ◦ ---

Laura watched Sebastian talking to a couple of people across the room. They had been invited to this party and decided to attend for a couple of hours. Laura sighed and glanced around the room. She recognized a lot of people but didn't know very many of them personally. Someone bumped into her, and she moved closer to the wall. "Excuse me." She murmured.

"*Excuse me.*" Said a voice as someone pushed closer to her.

Laura glanced up to see Dan standing beside her. She glanced back towards where Sebastian had been but didn't see him. "Please leave me alone, Dan." She pushed herself back as far against the wall as she could possibly get to get away from him.

"I just want to know what you think you are doing." Said Dan. "Do you really think that you can just rejoin this life? You're a has-been. It's been six years. Everyone will know you as a quitter."

"I've never left the industry, Dan."

Dan laughed. "I know. You're Matt Logan's assistant. That's a joke. A model being an agent's assistant. That dropped you down some didn't it? Did he feel sorry for you and hire you on out of pity?"

"What's wrong with you? I've never done anything to you. Why do you hate me so much?" Laura couldn't understand why Dan had such animosity towards her.

"I don't hate you, darling. I'd have to have some feelings for you. I just don't take kindly to know- it- all bitches who think that they can come into my studio and tell me how to run my movie. But I put you in your place." He leaned closer and lowered his face to hers. "And you liked it, didn't you?"

Laura cringed inside. Dan had so much hatred for her. She couldn't dare take her eyes off of him for fear of what he might do. But wait they were in public, so he couldn't do too much to draw attention to himself. She just had to figure out how to slip away from him.

"Laura." Jason walked up to them and nodded towards Dan. "Hi Dan."

Dan nodded at Jason as he pulled back from Laura. "Black."

Jason eyed Dan and Laura curiously and then turned towards Laura. "Sebastian's looking for you."

Laura pulled her eyes from Dan and glanced at Jason. "Thanks. I'm coming." She glanced back at Dan. "Excuse me."

Dan sneered at her and stepped back. Laura jumped away from the wall and moved over beside Jason. She glanced back to see Dan walking away and let out a breath. "Thanks for finding me."

Jason nodded and started walking, then stopped and turned towards her. "Sebastian cares about you."

"I know. I care about him, too." Answered Laura. "It's not what you think."

"I'm not sure what to think." Jason eyed her, watching her movements.

"I love Sebastian. I'd appreciate it if you didn't tell him that I was just talking to Dan."

"Why?" asked Jason.

"It would upset him, and I don't want him upset." Answered Laura.

"There you two are." Sebastian walked over to them and slid his arm around Laura's waist.

Laura smiled at Sebastian and glanced back at Jason.

"Are you ready to go?" asked Sebastian.

"If you are." Answered Laura.

"Jason?" asked Sebastian.

Jason eyed Laura. "I think I'll stick around here for a while longer. You two go ahead."

Sebastian nodded. "Okay. Let me tell Tanner that we are leaving."

"I'll be right there." Answered Laura as she watched Sebastian walk over to Tanner, who was the host of the party.

"I'll be quiet for now, but I will expect an explanation." Answered Jason.

Laura nodded. "Thank you." Great. Now she had to come up with an explanation for Jason. He thought that she was cheating on Sebastian. He couldn't be any further from the truth, but how did she tell him that without explaining everything about her past? When did life become so complicated? When she started dating Sebastian Thomas. The sneaking around, the secrets. Now it almost seemed worse. They had gone public with their relationship and there was still sneaking around and secrets. She had to find some kind of balance in her life, or she was going to go crazy. She hadn't even gone back home, yet. Who knew what kind of circus it would be there.

- - - ∾ - - -

Laura watched as Sebastian left and closed the door behind him, then sighed. She had to get out of this hotel room. She glanced at the clock and grabbed her cell phone. She dialed Mandy's number. She could meet her friend for lunch.

They used to do that all the time when they lived close to each other.

"Hello." Answered her friend.

"Hi. How about if I pick up lunch and meet you at your place? Do you have time?" asked Laura. She knew her words were running together, but she really needed to talk to her friend.

"What's wrong?" asked Mandy.

"I just want to have lunch." Answered Laura.

"I know that's not the whole truth. I'll meet you in an hour. You still have the key I gave you?"

"Yes." Laura reached for her purse. Mandy and she had traded keys to each other's places when they moved, so that if one ever arrived before the other, then they could go inside instead of waiting outside.

"See you then." Mandy hung up.

Laura hung up her phone and started going through her purse. She pulled out cash for cab fare and her debit card to buy lunch. She stuck Mandy's apartment key and her room key in her pocket along with her license and debit card, then grabbed a hat and sunglasses from her suitcase. She wrote a quick note to Sebastian telling him where she would be, grabbed her cell phone and then left the room. She had noticed the service elevators when she had went looking for ice, so she went to those and got lucky. One of the maids was just getting off of one and let her on. She took the elevator straight to the garage. She glanced around and then jumped when someone honked their horn. A car pulled up beside her and rolled down the window.

Rachel was laughing. "Sorry. I didn't mean to scare you. Need a ride?"

"I was heading to my friend's place over on 5th." Said Laura.

"I can give you a ride. Hop in."

"Thanks." Laura opened the door and slid into the passenger seat. "Are you finished for the day?"

Rachel shook her head. "No. I'm just going to meet my boyfriend for lunch."

"I don't want to make you late." Answered Laura.

"You won't. I always leave early." Answered Rachel as she pulled out of the parking garage. "Things have been kind of crazy since you and Sebastian went public, huh?"

Laura nodded. "Yes. I knew they would be but was hoping they would die down."

"You are a hot commodity now. People want to know what you did to get his attention." Rachel smiled as she pulled up in front of Mandy's apartment building. "Sebastian thinks you're special and that's what matters."

Laura smiled. "He's pretty great himself." She grabbed the door handle and slid her other hand into her pocket and pulled out some money. "Thanks for the ride."

"Don't even try it." Said Rachel. "Save it for cab fare later."

Laura laughed. "Thank you. Enjoy lunch with your boyfriend."

--- ❦ ---

Laura stepped out of the car and shut the door, then crossed the street to the deli. She got in line and eyed the board on the wall behind the counter. This was her and Mandy's favorite place to eat. She stepped up to the register.

"Good afternoon, ma'am. What can I get you?" asked the man behind the register, who had a name tag that read Henry.

Laura smiled at him. "I'll take a large Greek salad, extra feta, a turkey club and a piece of your double chocolate cake, please."

Henry glanced behind her. "That's not all for you?"

Laura laughed. "No. I'm picking up lunch for a friend." She handed him her card and watched as he swiped it, then handed her the card back with her receipt.

"It will be ready in a few minutes."

"Thank you." Said Laura as she stepped away from the counter and over to a bench nearby.

"Excuse me, ma'am."

Laura glanced up at the voice.

"Aren't you-?" The lady held up a magazine that she was reading that had Laura and Sebastian's picture on the front cover.

"Lady, read the sign." Henry pointed to a sign above the counter.

PLEASE DO NOT HARRASS MY CUSTOMERS
OR I WILL ASK YOU TO LEAVE.

"Oh!" The lady stepped back from Laura. "How rude." She glanced back at Laura and then at Henry.

"Lady, there's lots of celebrities that come in here. Why? Because they don't get bothered. If you don't like it- leave." Henry turned towards Laura. "Your order's ready, ma'am."

Laura walked up to the counter. "Thank you."

Another man stepped out of the office. "You were going to leave without saying hello?"

Laura smiled at the man that she'd known for eight years. "Frank. You were hiding in your office."

"You were out here stirring up trouble." He tipped his head towards the lady leaving the deli. "Scaring off my customers."

"Sorry."

"No problem. We've had the same policy for the last twenty years. That's why I'm still open. People can eat with the celebrities and just enjoy being in the same room as them or they can eat somewhere else."

Doesn't matter to me." He nodded towards the magazine rack. "You're getting back into the spotlight, I see."

"Yes- Sebastian. I'm really happy."

Frank nodded. "Good. Tell Mandy hello for me."

"I will."

Laura grabbed a couple magazines from the rack and signed the covers, then slid them and the money to cover the cost of the magazines across the counter. "For what it's worth. Thanks."

"Not necessary, but thanks." Said Frank. "It's worth a lot." He picked up the magazines off of the counter and glanced at them. "You two look good together."

"Thank you." Laura picked up her bag off the counter.

"Take care, Henry." She said to the man running the register, who nodded at her as she left the deli.

Chapter Thirteen

"Okay. Now that we've pigged out. Tell me what's going on." Said Mandy as she put empty containers in the empty bag from the deli.

Laura smiled weakly at her friend. "I'm going crazy. I don't know what I'm doing."

"What do you mean?"

"I ran into Dan again last night." Explained Laura.

"Again?" asked Mandy. "When else did you see him?"

"I ran into him at the hotel right after I got here. He thinks I enjoyed what he did to me. He thinks I want more from him. He was taunting me last night."

"Does Sebastian know?" asked Mandy, concerned.

"Sebastian actually walked up on Dan and me at the hotel. I swear Mandy, I don't know what would have happened if Sebastian hadn't shown up. I'd like to think that I could prevent it from ever happening again, but I just don't know if I could. Dan is vicious." Laura rushed through her explanation and wrung her hands in her lap.

"I didn't even know that you'd seen him, again. I've managed to stay away from him. I let other people handle his interviews."

"I'm sorry. I don't mean to dump this on you."

"Don't even go there. You know that you are not dumping this on me." Scolded Mandy.

"Jason saw Dan and me talking last night. If you could call it that. He seems to think that there's something going on between us."

"Did you set him straight?"

"Yes, but I also asked him not to say anything to Sebastian. Sebastian would kill Dan. You should have seen Dan last time. He was so mad." Laura looked at her friend, desperately. "What am I doing?"

Mandy moved to the couch and sat by her friend. "Do you love Sebastian?"

"You know I do."

"Then you are doing the right thing. Don't you worry. Dan will get his." Mandy hugged Laura. "Karma. Things always go full circle."

"Thanks, Mandy."

"Anytime."

--- ❧ ---

Laura glanced around as she stepped into the lobby. The service elevator required a key and no employees were around, so she'd have to walk through the front lobby. She noticed the crowd near the elevator and headed for the stairs. No way was she getting into the middle of that. She didn't feel like answering questions and dealing with reporters and Sebastian's fans. She entered the stairwell and took a breath. She glanced up. Maybe climbing the stairs would work off some of this nervous energy.

--- ❧ ---

Jason entered the lobby in time to see Laura enter the stairwell. He glanced around at the crowds and noticed Dan slip from the crowd and into the stairwell. Laura had said nothing was going on between them. So why were they meeting in the stairwell? He shrugged and started towards the door that he'd seen them enter. Only one way to find out.

--- ❦ ---

Laura paused and bent over to take a deep breath. What had she been thinking? Nine flights of stairs. She was only on the seventh floor. She moved over to the wall when she heard someone walking up behind her.

"Laura. We really have to quit meeting like this." Said Dan.

Laura stood up abruptly, feeling panicked, and started for the door.

Dan grabbed her and shoved her against the wall.

"Dan. What are you doing here?" asked Laura. How did he always manage to turn up when she was alone? Was he following her?

"I'm curious. What does Sebastian see in you?" Dan gripped her chin and tipped her head up. "Do you still just lie there, or do you participate?"

Laura jerked her head back. "Get away from me." She brought her knee up, but Dan had anticipated that and jerked out of the way, laughing. She tried to remain calm. If she lost it, he would win.

"I do remember that feisty attitude. That did make it more enjoyable." He shoved his knee between hers and pinned her to the wall.

"Why do you bother with me?" asked Laura. Maybe if she could get him talking, then someone would come along before he could try anything.

"Because you were the one that I couldn't bend to my will. I always get what I want. You have been the only exception." He smiled. "I did get some of what I wanted from you, though."

"You two seem to be inseparable." Said Jason as he walked up behind Dan.

Dan stepped back from Laura. "Black. What are you doing here?"

Jason glanced at Laura. "I don't trust Laura and thought that she was messing around on Sebastian. I guess now I have my answer."

Dan smiled. "Laura likes audiences. Do you want to watch or maybe join in?" Dan slid his hand to Laura's waist.

Jason watched Dan's hand and then glanced at Laura's face. She looked terrified. "Don't you have a room? I'm not much for public display."

Dan laughed. "I guess that means you don't mind getting a piece of this if she's stepping out on your buddy?" his hand moved to the button of Laura's jeans, then he glanced back at Jason.

Laura slapped Dan and caught him by surprise. She jerked free and ran for the stairs. "There is no way you are touching me, again."

Dan darted after Laura and caught her ankle as she made it halfway up the stairs. He pulled her leg and she instinctively put her right arm out and caught herself before she could slam her head into the concrete steps. Jason grabbed Dan and pulled him away from Laura.

"Did I understand correctly? Were you going to rape her?" asked Jason, furiously.

Dan looked at Jason. "She's just a little tramp. Surely, you're not going to fight me for her."

Jason glanced back at Laura, who was sitting on the top of the stairs, rubbing her right arm. "No. I'm not going to fight you for her." Jason pulled his arm back and punched Dan in the nose. "If you go near her, again, you'll regret it."

Dan stumbled back and grabbed his nose. "You'll never work on one of my films, again."

"Don't worry. I don't want to." Said Jason. He climbed the stairs to Laura and helped her stand. "Are you okay?"

Laura nodded. "I'm fine." She glanced back at Dan, who was tilting his head back and leaning against the wall.

"I'll see you to your room." Jason took her left arm and helped Laura up the last two flights of stairs, down the hall and into her room.

Laura sat on the couch and fought tears while Jason grabbed the box of tissues from the bathroom.

"You want to tell me what was going on?" asked Jason.

"I told you that I wasn't cheating on Sebastian, especially not with Dan." Laura explained.

"Yes. You did. But what is going on?"

"Nothing. Just please don't tell Sebastian."

"Laura, I don't even know what I'm not supposed to be telling Sebastian." Said Jason, exasperatedly.

"You can't tell him anything."

"Why not?" asked Jason.

Laura jumped off the couch and started pacing. "It's for his own good. Promise me. You won't tell him."

"Tell me why."

"Dan and I have a history. Sebastian knows about it."

"You used to date that jerk?" Jason eyed her speculatively.

Laura shook her head. "No. We didn't date." Laura walked to the closet. "Never mind. This is crazy. What was I thinking? I knew this would never work." She started packing things into her suitcase. She grabbed her toiletries from the bathroom and tossed them into her bag. She zipped up her bags and grabbed her purse. "I'm leaving. Tell Sebastian whatever you want."

Jason walked over to her and grabbed her right arm. "Tell me what's going on."

Laura jerked back and cried out, dropping her bags. Jason let go of her arm. "What's wrong?"

"I think I bruised it." Laura picked her bags back up, more carefully this time, and walked to the door.

Jason followed her. "At least let me give you a ride."

Laura turned and studied Jason. She seemed to wrestle with herself and then nodded. "Okay. Thank you."

They managed to sneak out to the garage by using the service elevators, again, then Laura called to change her flight. She closed her phone and turned to Jason. "Can you drop me off at the apartments on 5th?"

"Is that Mandy's place?" asked Jason.

"Yes." Answered Laura.

Jason nodded. "I guess going back to the hotel is not an option?" He glanced at her expression. "Okay."

A few minutes later, they stopped in front of Mandy's and slipped into a spot that had just been vacated. "I'll help you with your bags."

Laura knocked on the door, then let herself in. She knew Mandy wasn't home because she'd told her earlier that she was working late. Laura put her bags behind the couch and sat down. "Thank you for driving me."

Jason sat down beside her. "Laura. I want to understand what is going on. Are you just going to leave Sebastian and not say anything?"

"Did you really think that I was cheating on Sebastian?"

"I wasn't sure. All I know is that something isn't right with you. You had a promising future, then you dropped out of the spotlight for six years and started working as an agent assistant." Jason turned towards her. "You were good. I worked with you. What happened?"

Laura sighed. "I'll tell you if you promise not to tell Sebastian about Dan."

Jason shook his head. "I don't know if I can do that, Laura."

"Sebastian knows about my past. We don't have any secrets. If he knew that Dan was harassing me, then he'd go after him. I don't want anything to affect Sebastian's career." Pleaded Laura.

"Tell me."

"The short version is that Dan assaulted me and videotaped it. I never filed charges. I just dropped out of the public eye."

"I'm sorry."

"You understand, though, don't you? If Sebastian finds out, then– he just can't. Promise me you won't tell him." Said Laura.

"Are you really going to just leave him?" asked Jason.

Laura sighed and dropped her head into her hands. "I love Sebastian, but I was kidding myself to think that I could be with him. Dan will never let things go. Sebastian's better off without me. My flight leaves in the morning. I'll call Sebastian and tell him that I just can't handle all of the publicity."

Jason stood up, abruptly. "Wait. That's it. Don't do anything crazy. I'll be back in a couple of hours."

"You're not going to talk to Sebastian, are you?" asked Laura.

"No. I'm not going to talk to Sebastian."

"Okay. I'll be here." Laura agreed.

Jason walked to the door and then turned back to her. "Are you okay?"

Laura nodded and forced a smile. "I'm fine."

- - - ♋ - - -

As soon as Jason left, Laura let the tears fall. She cried in frustration and sadness. She didn't blame anyone but herself. She'd known from the beginning that it couldn't work. She should have just stayed away from Sebastian Thomas. But, she hadn't. Instead, she'd spent more and more time with him and let herself fall in love. She'd given him her heart and now she had to walk away. She might as well leave it with him. She'd never use it, again. Not after him. No one would ever compare to the man that she had fallen in love with. Yes, he was a well-known celebrity and handsome, but he was so much more. Funny, caring, fun to be with, kind, respectful, honest. But he couldn't be hers. She didn't deserve someone like him. She could only hurt his career and she didn't want to do that to him.

Laura's phone rang and she glanced at it. Not Sebastian. Matt. She grabbed a tissue and wiped her tears, then blew her nose before answering. "Hello."

"Hi, Laura. How is everything going?" asked Matt.

Laura smiled. "Everything's good here. How are you doing? Is the press horrible there?"

"No. It's not too bad. I held a small press conference, going by the article that Mandy wrote. It quieted everyone down mostly. There are questions about your modeling career, though." He paused and she heard Elizabeth in the background. "We knew there would be. I just wanted to check on you and see if you're still going to be gone for the rest of the week."

Laura sighed. She didn't want to tell Matt that she'd be home tomorrow. She wanted to hide for a while. Hopefully, she could slip into her apartment unnoticed. "I'm not sure, yet. Can I get back to you on that?"

"Is everything okay? You don't sound right." Said Matt.

Leave it to Matt to notice when she was lying. "Yes. Everything's fine. You just take care of you and Elizabeth. I'll call you later in the week. Tell Elizabeth Hi for me. Bye, Matt." Laura hung up her phone and set it on the table. She glanced at her clothes and decided to take a shower, then a nap.

Laura took a quick shower stand then curled up on Mandy's couch with a blanket. She was so exhausted after the day's events that she fell asleep rather quickly.

--- ☙ ---

Sebastian got back to the room and found the note from Laura. He glanced at his watch. It seemed awfully late for lunch. He dialed Laura's number, but she didn't answer. He decided to call Mandy's. Maybe he could meet up with them.

"Hello." Answered Mandy.

"Hi, Mandy. It's Sebastian. I was going to see if I could meet up with you and Laura." Sebastian explained.

Mandy glanced at the clock. "Laura and I had lunch hours ago."

Sebastian frowned, then noticed the closet open. Laura's clothes were gone. He walked into the bathroom and all of her things were gone from there, too. "When's the last time that you saw Laura?"

"Probably around one. She said that she was going back to the hotel." Answered Mandy. "Is something wrong?"

"All her things are gone." Answered Sebastian. "She left. Why would she do that?" Sebastian felt like he'd been punched in the gut. Things had been going great with him and Laura. Why would she just leave without telling him? Had Matt called her for something? Surely, there wasn't anything that urgent.

"Meet me at my place. 1323 5th Avenue. It's across from *Frank's Deli*." Said Mandy.

Sebastian sat down on the bed and grabbed a pen and paper, jotting down the address. "Okay."

"I'll be there as quickly as I can." Said Mandy.

--- ∞ ---

Jason walked to the security office and knocked on the door.

"Come in." the door buzzed, and he pushed it open and entered the dark room.

"What can I do for you Mr. Black?" The security guard turned towards him.

"How did you know it was me?" asked Jason, glancing at the monitors in front of him.

The guard smiled. "There's a camera over the door. I wouldn't have buzzed you in if I didn't recognize you. Also, I've seen every one of your action films. Dalton Powers is my favorite agent."

Jason smiled. "Thanks."

"So, what brings you here?" asked the guard.

Jason glanced at the guard's name tag. "Brian. Have you been working in here all day?"

"No, sir. I just came on about an hour ago. Why?"

"Can you see everything that goes on in the hotel from here?" asked Jason.

Brian shook his head. "Are you researching for a part?"

"Something like that." Answered Jason.

Brian nodded. "We have two cameras on each floor and one in each stairwell. Several behind the check-in desk and the lobby. We can monitor what's going on, but we don't see everything. The floor cameras rotate, and the stairwell cameras rotate. See this one." Brian pointed to a monitor for the third floor. "This monitor rotates between the two floor cameras and the stairwell camera."

"Do all the floor cameras do that?"

Brian nodded. "Yes. The only stationary monitors are the front desk and lobby. The rest all rotate."

"Do they record what's going on?"

"Yes. All the cameras record. The recordings are stationary, though. They don't cycle like the monitors. There's a CD for each camera for each day."

"So, it would be possible to look at a cd for the camera in stairwell seven for say around one-thirty?" asked Jason.

Brian eyed Jason, curiously. "Yes. Is that something I should be taking a look at?"

"Is there sound also?" asked Jason, avoiding the question, trying to come up with a good reason to get a copy of the CD and not arouse suspicion.

"Yes, there is sound. I have it turned down right now. It can get overwhelming, so we generally leave it off." Explained Brian.

"Any chance that I could get a copy of the cd for stairwell seven?" asked Jason.

"Is there something that I should know?" asked Brian.

"No. I promise there's no crime. I would be appreciative, though, if I could get a copy of it. So appreciative that I could send you a complete set of Dalton Powers *Night Mission* movies, all signed." Offered Jason.

Brian studied him. "There's no crime. So, if I was to look at the video for that time frame, I wouldn't feel the need to report anything to the police?"

Jason held his gaze. "There's no crime. You might feel the need to talk to the police, but you also might see how things could be handled privately."

Brian nodded as he pulled a blank CD out of a box and slid it in a player, then copied stairwell seven to it. He ejected the CD and slipped it into a plastic cover and handed it to Jason.

"Thank you." Jason accepted it and handed Brian a card. "If you'll call this number and ask for Mary, she'll take your address, so we can get the movies out to you."

Brian took the card. "Sure. Thanks. Let me know if I can do anything else for you."

Jason slipped the CD into his jacket pocket. "This is plenty. Thank you."

- - - ♋ - - -

Laura awoke to someone knocking on the door. She sat up and looked around, not sure why she was in Mandy's apartment, then remembered what happened. She walked to the door and peeked through the peep hole. Jason was standing on the other side of the door. She unlocked the door and Jason stepped inside. "Is everything okay? I've been knocking for a few minutes."

Laura nodded. "Sorry. I fell asleep on the couch."

"No problem." Jason glanced around the room. "Where's Mandy's DVD player?"

"I think she has one hooked up to this tv." Laura walked over to the media cabinet in Mandy's living room and opened the door. "Yes. Here's one. Why?"

Jason pulled the CD out of his jacket pocket and put it into the player and turned the tv on. "You said that Dan had a CD of you two."

"That's not a copy, is it?" asked Laura alarmed. "I don't want to see it."

Jason turned to Laura. "No. It's not a copy of that. It's video from the hotel."

"Oh." Laura sunk down onto the couch. "I don't know if I want to see this one, either."

Jason sat beside her. "I owe you an apology."

"No. It's okay. I probably would have thought the same thing." Said Laura.

"I didn't even give you a chance. I just assumed the worst. I'm sorry." Said Jason sincerely.

Laura smiled at him. "It's okay. Really. I'm glad Sebastian has such a good friend."

"I'm glad Sebastian met you."

Laura shook her head. "I'm still leaving tomorrow."

"Let's take a look at this video first before you make any snap decisions." Said Jason. He picked up the remote and pressed play. They watched the video for a few minutes and then fast forwarded it until right before the time that they were in the stairwell. They saw Laura climb the stairs and stop in the stairwell.

Laura turned around as she heard the knob of the front door. "Stop it. I don't want Mandy to see it." Laura stood up as Mandy and Sebastian walked in.

Jason hit the stop button and stood up beside Laura.

"Laura? I thought you went back to the hotel. What's going on?" asked Mandy, glancing around the room. She eyed her friend and Jason speculatively.

Laura forced a smile for her friend. "I was going to talk to you when you got home."

"Well, I'm home." Prodded Mandy.

"Why did you pack all of your things?" interrupted Sebastian. "Are you leaving?"

Jason walked over to the media cabinet and casually closed the door.

Mandy shook her head. "I don't think so. Let's see what you're trying to hide." Mandy opened the door and hit play on the DVD player.

They all watched as Laura stood in the stairwell and then Dan came up behind her and shoved her up against the wall.

"He came after you, again?" asked Mandy.

Laura sank down onto the couch and swallowed, trying not to cry. She looked at the floor, not wanting to look at the tv. She didn't want to see what happened. It was already replaying in her head.

Sebastian glanced from Mandy to Laura. "Again, as in since the hotel incident or has there been others?"

Laura refused to look at Sebastian. "I told you from the beginning that this wouldn't work. I tried to tell you all along, but you wouldn't listen. Dan won't let it go. I'm just going to go back to my life in Savannah. You have your life here. It will be better that way."

Sebastian looked at Laura incredulously. "Like hell. I love you. We are happy together. I am not going to let Dan ruin that."

"It's my decision, Sebastian. I can make it." Answered Laura.

"I don't get a choice in the matter?" asked Sebastian. He strode over to Laura and dropped beside her on the couch.

"We talked about this already. We agreed that if it wasn't working, we'd part ways." Laura said. She glanced up at Sebastian. "I can't lie and say I don't love you because I do, but this is the best thing that I can do for us. For you."

Sebastian grabbed Laura's arm and she cried out. He let go and glanced at the video.

"He did this to you." Sebastian stood up and glanced at Jason. "Thank you for helping her when I was not there to do so."

Jason ejected the CD and nodded at Sebastian.

Mandy knelt down and looked at Laura's arm. She touched it gently and watched Laura's facial expressions. "I think you need to go to the hospital. You might have broken it."

Laura shook her head. "It's fine."

Sebastian walked around Laura and bent down and picked her up from the opposite side, so that her injured arm was away from him. "Jason– get your car. Mandy- get Laura's purse." He growled, then walked to the door.

"Sebastian. Put me down." Laura said exasperatedly. She glanced up into his scowling face. "You can't manhandle me."

"I intend to do a lot more than that." Stated Sebastian.

- - - ❦ - - -

Laura sat in the emergency room, surrounded by Jason, Mandy and Sebastian. She tried not to smile. She really wanted to cry. She was here because of Dan. Sebastian wouldn't let her go. She was quietly pleased that Sebastian loved her enough to tell her no. She really didn't want to leave him. She loved Sebastian so much. She just wasn't sure that she could be in his world. Sure, she was in the entertainment industry, but she had a quieter life. A much more private life. She would never have that with Sebastian. She had always felt for the celebrities who never caused problems and were never rowdy in public, yet their pictures would end up on the cover because someone got a picture of them looking less than perfect. Or someone would analyze why they'd been married for so long and were they secretly having an affair? It didn't matter if you had any skeletons or not, they always found something to say about you- true or not.

A doctor stepped into her makeshift room. "Ms. Steele. I'm Dr. Bowman." He glanced around. "Well, four celebrities in one room." He held up her x-rays. "I've looked these over and if you notice right here. You have a distal radius fracture." He smiled at the concerned looks. "A fracture in your wrist bone. This is a common fracture. People tend to try to break their fall with their hands and unfortunately, they get a fractured wrist. There are two treatment options. We can put a cast on it or just put a splint on your arm and give you a sling. The fracture is so small that it should heal properly on its own, but if you are going to have a hard time keeping it in a sling, then we should put it in a cast."

"A splint will be fine. How long will it take to heal?" asked Laura.

"About six weeks if you keep it in the sling and don't use it." Answered the doctor.

- - - ❦ - - -

Sebastian sat beside Laura on the couch. They had all gone back to Mandy's after the hospital. Mandy and Jason had gone out to pick up takeout and Laura and Sebastian were now alone. Sebastian turned towards Laura. "I want you to file charges against Dan."

Laura shook her head. "No. That will bring all kinds of publicity."

"I don't care about the publicity. He has cornered you three times and he needs to be held accountable."

"I'm fine."

"Says the woman with her arm in a sling." Remarked Sebastian.

"Just let it go." Said Laura.

"No. I will not let this go. I am tired of him thinking that he can do whatever he wants to whomever he wants. What if he is harassing other women? Have you thought about that? He got away with it once, why not try again?"

"We would have heard about that."

"Not if they are reacting like you and not telling anyone."

Laura looked down at her hands. Sebastian turned her chin towards him. "I love you and I hate that he did this to you. I want to do something. He is not going to keep harassing you. If you won't file charges, I'll deal with him myself."

Laura jumped up alarmed and started pacing. "You can't. He'll make something up and try to ruin your career. Just leave him alone."

Sebastian stood up and walked over to her. "We can't let him keep doing this to you. He has made you scared to live. Do you really think that you can just go back to Savannah and hide out?"

"Yes."

Sebastian shook his head and gave her a weak smile. "You do not actually think that you can just hide now. Everyone knows that we are together. There will be speculation and you might not like whatever they come up with. Why don't we just tell them the truth? Won't that be better?"

Laura dropped on to the couch and sighed. "I don't want to tell anyone anything."

Sebastian wrapped his arms around her. "I know baby, but we do not have that choice now. If you run away and try to hide, everyone will wonder why. Eventually, something will come out."

Chapter Fourteen

"Maybe we should leak the video to the press." Said Jason. He and Sebastian were having lunch a few days after Laura had left for home.

Sebastian glowered at his friend. "No. Don't mention that, again."

Jason shrugged. "Fine, but I've heard rumors that Laura's not the only one that Dan has been crossing the line with."

"From where?" asked Sebastian.

"I heard a couple of the Assistant Directors talking the other day. They said that Dan was scaring away the talent because he makes unreasonable demands and that a couple girls have quit his films because he made passes at them."

"Why isn't any of this in the tabloids?" asked Sebastian.

Jason shook his head. "I don't know. Maybe they are scared like Laura."

Sebastian balled up his fists in frustration. "I hate this. There has to be something we can do."

"I told you what I thought." Answered Jason.

"No." snapped Sebastian.

--- ❧ ---

Laura glanced out her window and scanned the parking lot. She'd been home for almost a week now and almost every day someone had been parked outside her apartment. Today, the parking lot looked empty. Her phone rang and she jumped. She sighed in frustration and hurried to the kitchen to answer it. She hated being jumpy all of the time.

"Laura. Turn on the television. Now." Mandy told her.

"Hello to you, too." Said Laura as she grabbed her remote.

"Sorry, but you're going to want to see this." Apologized Mandy. "Turn to *Entertainment Update*."

Laura turned on the tv and flipped through the channels until she came to *Entertainment Update*, then she dropped the remote and sank down onto the couch. "How? Where? Surely Jason didn't–"

"I doubt it was Jason, but somebody leaked the video." Responded Mandy sympathetically.

Laura sat in shock while the video of Dan assaulting her in the stairwell of the hotel played across the screen. She wasn't sure if it was lucky or not that there was no audio. The video ended and Marla Snow came onto the screen.

"Well, an interesting turn of events. Is Sebastian Thomas's Laura having a fling with his director? What do you think Jason Black was doing there?" she paused dramatically. *"Tune in tomorrow for the story."*

The credits started rolling and Laura flopped back onto the couch. What was she going to do now?

"Laura! Are you still there?" yelled Mandy.

Laura looked at her hands, realized that she was still holding the phone and put it up to her ear. "Sorry, Mandy. I don't know what to say."

"Don't say anything. Call Matt in case he hasn't seen it and see if you can hide at his place. Don't go to work and get out of your apartment. Call me when you get somewhere. We'll figure this out."

Laura turned off the tv. "Okay. I'll talk to you later."

Laura sat on the couch, staring at the blank tv screen until someone knocked on the door. Then she jumped into action. She rushed to the door and peeked out of the peep hole, then sighed when she saw Elizabeth. She opened the door.

"Do you have your bag packed? Matt called and said to pick you up immediately. Something was leaked to the press, and he said you needed to get out of your apartment."

Elizabeth entered the apartment and stopped halfway down the hall when she realized that Laura was still standing with the door open. "Laura. Close the door. Come on. We don't have much time. If any."

Laura nodded and shut the door, then rushed to her room and grabbed a bag from the closet.

Elizabeth started packing the things in her bathroom. "You can call Sebastian on the way."

Laura zipped her bag closed and grabbed another one. "Sebastian is in a closed shoot. I can't call him."

"Matt will know how to reach him. Or Walter." She grabbed Laura's phone charger and laptop off the desk and shoved them in a bag. "Anything else, we'll pick up."

She grabbed Laura's bags and pulled her to the door. She looked out the living room window and let out a groan, then ran back to the door and opened it to peek out. She saw the vans and crew pull up in the parking lot, so she pulled Laura behind her and down the back stairs.

"I parked on the other side of this park. Hopefully, we can get away unnoticed." Elizabeth glanced both ways at the foot of the stairs and then started across the park that was directly behind Laura's apartment, keeping to the trees, hoping they didn't get noticed before they got to the other side. They tossed the bags into the car and drove out of the apartment complex, passing news vans along the way.

--- ❦ ---

Laura glanced around as they pulled up to the docks. "Why are we here?"

Matt walked over to the car and opened the door for Elizabeth. He kissed her and they talked briefly, then he walked to Laura's side and opened the passenger door.

Laura stepped out of the car. "Why are we here?" she repeated.

"We're going to hide you on my boat for a couple days. There's plenty of food and I don't think anyone will think to look for you here." Answered Matt.

"But– I-" Laura just stopped mid-sentence and sighed. "How come you are prepared for this? I wasn't."

Matt smiled at Laura. "It was Elizabeth's idea. We knew that they'd try your apartment and the agency. Possibly even our place, but they probably won't think of the boat."

"Thank you." Said Laura appreciatively as everyone grabbed her bags and carried them towards the boat.

"Now, you know how to drive her and run everything. You've been out on her enough, so I think you'll be fine. If you don't see us for a few days, then we can't sneak away. There's plenty of food for at least a week. It's your choice if you want to stay in the docks or go out, but just remember that you can't be seen on the docks in case someone is looking for you out here." Explained Matt, then he glanced at her arm, in a sling. "What am I thinking? You can't drive like that." He glanced at Elizabeth.

Elizabeth nodded. "Let me take care of a couple of things and then I'll be back. I'll keep you company." She looked at Laura.

Laura nodded, reluctantly. "Okay. Thank you."

--- ❦ ---

"You're somewhere safe?" asked Mandy.

"Yes. I-"

"Don't tell me. Not right now. I'll try to find out what's going on and get information to you. Just lay low, okay?" Mandy paused as there was a beep on her phone. "Hold on." She glanced at her caller id and switched calls. "Victoria. Hi."

"What is going on?" asked Victoria. "Are you holding out on me?"

Mandy sat up straight. "What do you mean?"

"I've heard that *Entertainment Update* has some exclusive news about Sebastian and Laura. Why don't we have it since you are Laura's best friend?" demanded Victoria.

"I don't know what you mean." Responded Mandy. "I haven't heard anything."

"Well, you'd better find out. I don't like being scooped." Said Victoria, then she hung up.

Mandy sighed and switched back to Laura. "I'll call you back soon, okay?"

--- ∽ ---

Sebastian went to his dressing room to change. Finally, the re-shoots were completed. He wanted to call Laura and see how she was doing. He stepped into his dressing room and found Walter waiting for him inside.

"Walter, what are you doing here?" asked Sebastian, curiously.

"I wanted to let you know what's going on before you hear it from someone else." Answered Walter.

Sebastian immediately stopped what he was doing and gave Walter his full attention. "What has happened?"

Walter shook his head. "Really, Sebastian, I wish you two would have told me what was going on. Now, I have to figure out how to handle this."

"Handle what Walter?"

"There's been a video leaked. Actually sold to *Entertainment Update*."

"Of what?" demanded Sebastian.

Walter studied Sebastian. "I hope that doesn't mean there's more than one video."

"Walter." Prompted Sebastian.

Walter nodded. "Laura and Dan in the stairwell. Jason interrupting something. There's speculation that she's having an affair or that he's assaulting her."

"Damnit!" Sebastian reached for his phone, but Walter grabbed it from him.

"Tell me what is going on, so I can help you handle this."

Sebastian studied his agent and friend for a few minutes and then nodded. "Okay." He gestured to a chair and sat down opposite it. "Have a seat."

--- ❧ ---

As soon as Walter sat, Sebastian told him the whole story of Dan and Laura. Walter listened quietly and nodded occasionally.

"Well, that explains a lot." Said Walter. "Where's Laura now?"

Sebastian shook his head. "I don't know. If she saw the show, hopefully, not at her apartment. "I am sure Matt is helping her hide. I need to call and check on her."

"How do you think she will handle this?" asked Walter.

"I don't know that, either. She has been hiding from this for six years." Answered Sebastian.

"Maybe it's time that it came out." Said Walter.

"Maybe. I need to make a couple calls."

Walter nodded." Okay. Check on her. We'll talk about things afterwards."

Sebastian nodded and grabbed his phone.

Laura answered immediately. "Hello."

"Are you okay?" asked Sebastian in relief.

"Yes. Matt took care of everything. I left my apartment as soon as I saw it on tv. It will be worse tomorrow, though. They're claiming to have the whole story."

"We will see about that." Said Sebastian. "Let me check on some things and I will call you back."

"Okay."

"I love you."

"Still? After all this mess?"

"Of course. I will call you back soon."

--- ❦ ---

Laura hung up her phone and sighed. What was she doing? Mandy and Sebastian had both called her and said they would find out what was going on and instructed her to hide out. Elizabeth and Matt took precautions to pick her up and hide her out. Was this what her life was going to be like? Did everyone think that she was this fragile?

Laura thought back over the last few years. She'd had a rough time when Dan had assaulted her, but she'd gotten through it. Yes, but she quit her career and moved to another one. That was okay. Her friends had helped her through everything. She was happy working at the agency. She had been happy in her other career, also.

She needed to be in control of her own life. Did she want to stay with Sebastian? Yes. Then she'd better learn how to handle a life in the spotlight. Any time something happened, it could be leaked. She would have to learn to live with it or walk away from Sebastian for good. It was about time that she stepped up and helped herself. It was about time that she got past this situation with Dan. He could only hurt her if she let him.

--- ❦ ---

Sebastian punched in the next number and listened to the phone ringing on the other end. "Hello?"

"Tell me you did not leak the video." Demanded Sebastian.

"No. I wouldn't do that, and you know it." Answered Jason.

Sebastian sighed. "I know. I just had to make sure. Someone sold the video to EU."

Jason cursed. "Let's go back to the source."

"Good idea." Answered Sebastian.

"What else are you going to do? The story's out now." asked Jason.

"I know. We will have to put out our own statement or let the speculation run its course."

"Sounds like you'd better talk to Laura."

"I will. Can you check with the guard at the hotel and let me know what you find out?"

"I'll call you back as soon as I know something."

"Thank you." Said Sebastian.

"No problem. Go take care of your girl." Said Jason.

--- ↶ ---

Sebastian hung up with Jason and sat down.

"What are you going to do now?" asked Walter.

Sebastian shook his head. "I'm not sure what to do. I don't think that Laura will talk about any of this and I don't know what their story will be tomorrow night."

"You need to talk to her about this. She needs to tell her side."

"I am not going to push her on this. It caused her a lot of damage– mentally and physically."

"It will only get worse if it isn't handled." Said Walter.

"I know." Sighed Sebastian.

--- ❧ ---

Laura sat on the boat and glanced around the docks. Not very much activity going on. There were only a few people around. Mostly only people that lived on their boats. What was the best way for her to handle this? Should she just do an interview and out Dan. He had a video, an edited video. It would be his word against hers. She shook her head. How would this affect Sebastian? Would it turn people away from him because he was associated with her? What would everyone think of her? Would she be a victim or a slut? How would it affect her friends? Especially Matt, Elizabeth and Mandy? They had stood by her through it all. Laura jumped up and started pacing on the boat. She would go crazy like this. She couldn't account for every possibility.

Laura grabbed her cell phone and dialed Mandy.

"Hello. Laura, is everything okay?" asked Mandy concerned. "I haven't found out anything, yet."

"Would you be interested in telling my side of the story?" asked Laura.

Mandy was quiet for a few moments. "What do you mean?"

"I guess first I should ask if it's okay with you if I tell my story?" said Laura.

"Laura. You do not need to ask my permission. If you want to talk about what happened to you that is your decision. Are you sure?"

Laura gripped the phone tighter and thought for a minute. "Yes. I'm sure. I just don't want anything to affect you."

Mandy sighed. "Laura, this isn't about me. This is about you. What Dan did to you was wrong and he should be held accountable. You don't need to worry about me. Just yourself. Okay?"

Laura smiled. "You are such an awesome friend."

"You're just now figuring that out? You're behind, girl." Mandy laughed. "How do you want to do this?"

"I'm not sure. Is it possible to get this out before *Entertainment Update*? I have no idea what story they have, but it can't be right."

"The best thing that I can think of is to do a phone interview. Then we can get the article out first thing in the morning. I'm sure Victoria will hold the paper for this."

"Okay. Will you check on that for me? I need to call Sebastian. I haven't talked to him about this, yet."

"Do you want me to wait to talk to Victoria until after you've talked to Sebastian?" asked Mandy.

"No. He's been trying to get me to press charges against Dan. I don't think he'll care if I tell my story."

"Okay. I'll talk to Victoria and then wait for your call."

Laura hung up her phone and took a breath, then dialed Sebastian's number.

--- ❦ ---

Sebastian glanced down at his phone buzzing and answered it immediately. "Laura. Is everything okay?"

"I hope so." Answered Laura. There was a brief pause. "I've decided to let Mandy interview me and tell my story about Dan."

Sebastian glanced at Walter. "About what happened in the stairwell?" he asked curiously.

"Everything. Why I left my modeling career. What happened on set. The threats. What happened when I visited you in LA. All of it."

Sebastian smiled. Did this mean that Laura was ready to move on? He had been hoping to help her get past this and it seemed now she was ready.

"Sebastian? Are you okay with this?" asked Laura uncertainly.

"Yes. I am. Are you sure? I don't want you to feel pressured into doing this."

"I'm sure. I need to take control of my own life. I'm ready to do this."

"Okay. How are you going to do it?"

"Mandy is thinking a phone interview, so it can go in tomorrow's paper and be out before *Entertainment Update's* episode airs."

"Okay. I will be there as soon as I can. Where will you be?"

"Right now. I'm on Matt's boat. Probably his place."

"I love you and I am proud of you." Said Sebastian.

"I love you, too. You might not be so proud when this is all out and we are being scrutinized."

"Whatever happens, we can handle it. I will see you soon." Sebastian hung up his phone. "I need to catch the next flight to Savannah."

"Don't you think that it would be better if she came here? You two are going to need to do a couple interviews after this story hits." Said Walter.

Sebastian looked at Walter. "You have a point, but I need to get to her before this hits tomorrow."

"Call Matt and get her a flight here. I will meet her at the airport and make sure she gets here okay."

Sebastian nodded and dialed Matt's number.

- - - ∾ - - -

Elizabeth boarded the boat carrying a duffel bag. "You ready to go out?"

Laura shook her head and smiled at her friend. Elizabeth was dressed in jeans and a blouse with tennis shoes. Not her usual attire. Elizabeth always wore slacks or dresses and looked very sophisticated. Of course, she had that air of sophistication even wearing jeans.

"We need to go to your place." Said Laura. "I hope you and Matt don't get too upset with me. I've decided to do an interview with Mandy and get the whole story out."

"Why would we be mad at you?" asked Elizabeth.

"This is going to bring a lot of unwanted attention to you guys and I hope it doesn't affect the agency." Explained Laura.

Elizabeth frowned. "I don't know how it could affect the agency, but I guess that's always a possibility." She studied Laura. "Are you sure? I don't know all of the details, but from what I do know, this won't be easy."

Laura nodded. "I'm sure. I need to do this."

"Okay, then. Let's go."

--- ☙ ---

"Matt, this is Sebastian."

"Are you looking for Laura? I've got her out on the boat." Answered Matt.

"Actually, she's probably on her way there. I need you to get her to the airport to fly to LA as soon as possible. I'll have a ticket waiting for her."

"Why? What's going on?" asked Matt, concerned.

"I'm sure she'll be calling you, but she's decided to do an interview with *LA Info*. I just want to get her here before it hits the stands."

"She's going to tell everything? Are you sure that's a good idea? Are you pushing her to do this?" demanded Matt.

"No. This was her idea."

"I don't know if it's a good one. Why didn't you talk her out of it?"

"Because she needs this. She needs to get past this."

"You mean you need for her to get past this. I was worried that you might pressure her."

"Matt. I love her. I only want what is best for her. She will never be happy until she can get past this. I know that it will never go away, but she needs to move on. She can't live in fear all of the time. You know what Dan is capable of. Look what he did to her the last time that they saw each other."

"I only want what is best for her, Sebastian."

"Then support her in this. She will need all the support that she can get."

"Okay. I'll get her to her flight, but you better take care of her while she is there."

"You have my word."

Chapter Fifteen

LA INFO

LAURA STEELE TELLS ALL

By Amanda Knight

Many of you know Laura Steele as the woman who caught Sebastian Thomas's heart. There's another Laura Steele that everyone remembers. Laura Steele was a supermodel and actress in 2005. Her career was soaring, and everyone wanted her. She couldn't accept half of the jobs offered and could pick and choose to do whatever she wanted. She had one of the fastest growing careers of any young model or actress to date. Just as her career was taking off, she disappeared from the limelight.

She still worked at Studio B with Matt Logan, but she worked as his assistant and stayed behind the scenes. Everyone wondered why she would give up such a promising career. Why she would settle for less. If you asked any of her friends, they would always say that Laura was happier doing what she was doing. That she didn't like being in the spotlight.

As the years went by, people would offer her jobs every once in a while, but she would politely decline. If by chance, you saw her in an ad, it was only for back up because they needed someone last minute. Everyone has wondered why she gave up her promising career. Now everyone will get their answers.

I recently had the opportunity to talk to Laura and she had a story to tell. The true story of her life.

Laura was interested in modeling in high school and college. She did modeling jobs to pay her way through college. When she graduated, she modeled full time and was offered numerous contracts. Matt Logan of Studio B was her agent and he also helped her get her first acting job. She was in several movies including 'Raven's Prey', 'Fallen', 'Lost Girl' and 'Second Chance Love' to name a few. She was finally cast in a lead role in a film titled 'Lover's Secret'. This film changed the path of Laura's life.

Laura always showed up early to rehearse and practice before filming began. She had a particular scene that was bothering her. If any of you have seen the movie, then you know that Laura was not in it.

However, she was cast in the role of Violet. For any of you who haven't seen the movie, this was the best friend who got caught in bed with her best friend's fiancée. Laura had a problem with this scene. First, she didn't want to be nude, so she requested to wear underwear. This caused problems with the directors of the movie. There were three at the time. Two agreed and one finally, reluctantly agreed, but wasn't happy about it.

He made sure that Laura knew how unhappy he was. He caught her at the studio when she was rehearsing and raped and beat her. Laura had a fractured wrist, two broken ribs and bruises over her entire face and body. She quit acting and modeling and stayed out of the spotlight altogether. She chose to work in the background and stay behind the scenes.

That was of course, until she met Sebastian Thomas. I'm sure everyone has seen the video previewed on Entertainment Update. Laura doesn't deny that the video is real. It seems that some people hold grudges- even after six years.

About three weeks ago, Laura flew to LA to spend time with Sebastian Thomas. What she wasn't expecting was to be cornered and assaulted by her old director. We have numerous witnesses who saw Laura get assaulted at the hotel where she and Sebastian were staying, not once, but twice. The video that you have seen was her being attacked by the same director who assaulted her six years ago. He was interrupted by Sebastian Thomas's best friend, Jason Black. Laura was lucky to get away from him this time with only a fractured wrist.

Why is she speaking out now? Because of the video some might say. Laura doesn't deny that the video instigated it, but she has told me that she needs to move on with her life. She is happy with Sebastian Thomas. She is happy with her job. She wants to get past this incident and move forward with her life with Sebastian.

"I don't want to be afraid anymore. I don't want to always be looking over my shoulder. The one thing that I would like to say to anyone who has been assaulted or raped is to tell someone. Report it. Don't let it rule your life. It will never go away, but you can live a healthier, happier life if you aren't always afraid of what might happen. I wish I would have listened to my friends when they told me to report my assault." *This is a direct quote from Laura.*

I saw the video and it is pretty clear to me who is in it, but for clarification— Laura Steele, Jason Black and Dan Morris.

Laura has not shown any interest in getting back into acting or modeling. She just felt it was time for her story to come out. She hopes that others will learn from what has happened to her.

Laura dropped the paper and leaned back against Sebastian. She tilted her head back and looked up at him "Last chance to get out before all hell breaks loose."

Sebastian looked down into her eyes. "Not a chance."

Laura sighed and turned around to look at him. "I'm serious, Sebastian. If you wanted to walk away now, no one would blame you. I certainly wouldn't blame you. Tyler was probably smart to distance himself from me."

Sebastian snorted derisively. "Tyler was a weasel and a coward. I am not going anywhere. Especially not because of something that happened to you in the past that you had no control over."

"I-" Sebastian leaned forward and interrupted her, pressing his lips to hers and kissing her. "End of discussion."

Laura opened her mouth to speak again and Sebastian returned his mouth to hers, effectively stopping any more of the conversation. Laura sighed into his mouth and relaxed into him. No more fighting. No more pushing him away. She had told him everything and given him the chance to leave. She smiled. He wasn't leaving.

Sebastian pulled back and looked at her. "Are you smiling? Is my kissing amusing?"

Laura laughed and pulled him closer. "I'm happy because you aren't leaving me."

Sebastian let out a heavy sigh and rolled his eyes heavenward. "Finally. She gets it."

Laura giggled and wound her arms around him, then pulled him over as she fell back onto the bed. "I love you, Sebastian."

"I love you, too."

Epilogue

LA INFO

THE TRUTH ALWAYS COMES OUT

By Amanda Knight

It appears that someone's been very busy. Since, Laura Steele told her story last week, several women have stepped forward and admitted that Dan Morris assaulted them, as well. Numerous women have said that he threatened them, and they walked out on roles for fear of what he might do. Laura Steele's assault cannot be prosecuted because the statute of limitations has expired, but for the others that have stepped forward, Dan Morris will answer for his crimes. No one is above the law. No one should be able to abuse their position the way that Dan Morris has done. As I told a friend, recently, everyone always gets what they deserve.

Dan Morris may have been a talented director, but he doesn't appear to be a people person. 'The second installment of Worlds Apart' will be offered to a new director and filming will start summer of next year.

As always, Thank you for Reading!

"Anyone affected by sexual assault, whether it happened to you or someone you care about, can find support by calling the National Sexual Assault Hotline at 800.656. HOPE (4673) to be connected with someone over the phone who can help."

www.ingramcontent.com/pod-product-compliance
Lightning Source LLC
Chambersburg PA
CBHW021548310726
48972CB00003B/733